MRS. MALORY
AND NO CURE
FOR DEATH

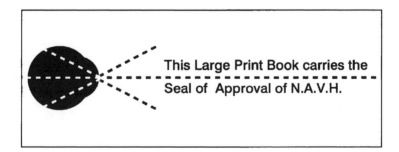

MRS. MALORY AND NO CURE FOR DEATH

A Sheila Malory Mystery

Hazel Holt

Thorndike Press • Waterville, Maine

Copyright © Hazel Holt, 2005

Published in 2006 by arrangement with NAL Signet, a division of Penguin Group (USA) Inc.

Thorndike Press® Large Print Mystery.

The tree indicium is a trademark of Thorndike Press.

The text of this Large Print edition is unabridged.
Other aspects of the book may vary from the original edition.

Set in 16 pt. Plantin by Christina S. Huff.

Printed in the United States on permanent paper.

Library of Congress Cataloging-in-Publication Data

Holt, Hazel, 1928–
    Mrs. Malory and no cure for death : a Sheila Malory mystery / by Hazel Holt.
        p. cm. — (Thorndike Press large print mystery)
    ISBN 0-7862-8344-0 (lg. print : hc : alk. paper)
    1. Malory, Sheila (Fictitious character) — Fiction.
2. Physicians — Crimes against — Fiction.   3. Women
detectives — England — Fiction.   4. England — Fiction.
5. Large type books.   I. Title.   II. Series: Thorndike Press
large print mystery series.
PR6058.O473M754 2006
823′.914—dc22   2005031437

For
Dr. Jan Fergus and Fr. Gabriel Myers, OSB
dear friends and fellow CMY enthusiasts

As the Founder/CEO of NAVH, the only national health agency solely devoted to those who, although not totally blind, have an eye disease which could lead to serious visual impairment, I am pleased to recognize Thorndike Press* as one of the leading publishers in the large print field.

Founded in 1954 in San Francisco to prepare large print textbooks for partially seeing children, NAVH became the pioneer and standard setting agency in the preparation of large type.

Today, those publishers who meet our standards carry the prestigious "Seal of Approval" indicating high quality large print. We are delighted that Thorndike Press is one of the publishers whose titles meet these standards. We are also pleased to recognize the significant contribution Thorndike Press is making in this important and growing field.

Lorraine H. Marchi, L.H.D.
Founder/CEO
NAVH

* Thorndike Press encompasses the following imprints: Thorndike, Wheeler, Walker and Large Print Press.

Chapter One

"I must say I do feel a fool," I said to Rosemary when she came round to sympathize. "It was such a stupid thing to do."

"What happened?" Rosemary asked.

"I suppose there was some water on the floor — I'd been draining the potatoes — and I was wearing an old pair of slippers, and the soles are a bit shiny, so I simply skidded across the kitchen floor and *crashed* into the work top and banged my wrist really hard."

"How awful. It must have been very painful."

"It was. Dreadful. I thought I'd just bruised it and put some arnica on, but it was still pretty miserable the next morning. Anyway, Michael came round to bring me some early peas from their garden and, being a dutiful son, insisted on taking me to Casualty to have it x-rayed. They said it was fractured and put this horrible plaster on."

"Oh, poor you. How wretched."

"It's not as bad as it might be. They left

my fingers free so I can pick things up, but I can't move anything heavy."

I moved over to put the kettle on, but Rosemary forestalled me.

"No, let me." She plugged it in and got out the cups and things. "How are you managing?"

"Not too bad. Michael and Thea wanted me to go and stay with them until the plaster's off, but I said no. I can cope, more or less, and it would be difficult with the animals. Which reminds me, could you open a couple of tins of food for them? I forgot to ask Thea when she was here — she comes in every day, bless her — and I do find those ring-pull cans awkward."

"Of course. How long have you got to keep the plaster on?"

"I've got to go back in a fortnight and they'll see how it's going. Thank heavens it's my left wrist — I'm dreadfully right-handed and I couldn't have coped if that one had gone."

"Well, for goodness' sake let me know if I can do anything. What about shopping?"

"I can drive short distances, so I can get to the shops."

"What about taking Tris for walks? I can easily take him when I take Alpha — they get on perfectly well together."

"It's sweet of you to offer, but he's getting on a bit and doesn't need a lot of exercise, so he's all right running about in the garden while the weather's fine."

"Well, just say, won't you?"

"It's Foss who's the trouble. He refuses to believe that I could have anything wrong with me that might interfere with *his* comfort!"

As if on cue, there was a thump as of a cat jumping off a bed, followed by the sound of a little light claw sharpening on the stair carpet, and Foss strolled into the kitchen demanding food.

"You see!" I said.

Rosemary smiled and opened a tin of cat food, spooned some out into a dish and put it down for Foss, who cleared the dish rapidly and looked up for more.

"He's pretending to be starving because you're here," I said. "Normally he only picks at that particular cat food."

"Shall I pour the tea?" Rosemary asked.

"Oh, yes, please. And there are some biscuits in that blue tin."

Foss, seeing that he had lost our attention, moved off into the sitting room.

"So," Rosemary said. "What exactly have you broken, did they say?"

"Oh, it's not bad — a hairline fracture of the radius, apparently."

"Oh, yes — the ulna and the radius, I remember them from Biology!"

"How clever of you. I don't remember *anything* from Biology. I was terrified of Miss Udall — she was so sarcastic. I always sat at the back and tried to keep my head down and out of her sight! Thank goodness I only had to do it for one year — I simply couldn't have got to the stage where you had to cut up frogs."

"Mm, she was formidable, wasn't she? Mind you, the science people said she was an absolutely brilliant teacher."

"Possibly, but details of the ulna and radius have passed me by. I was only glad to know it wasn't serious. Which reminds me. I saw poor Alan Johnson when I was at the hospital. He was just going in to have some more tests — his heart's playing up again. He looked awful, so I really can't complain about a hairline fracture, however inconvenient."

"Anyway," Rosemary said, "let me know if there's anything I can do."

It's funny the sort of things you can't do with only one usable hand, things you've always taken for granted. I couldn't get into certain garments (trousers and tights were a problem, so I was glad the weather was warm), I found I was using the microwave quite a bit since preparing food was difficult, and I found it very tiresome to have to remember to put a plastic bag over my hand and wrist when I was washing or washing up. And all the things everyone has always said about the misery of itching under the plaster (scratching with a knitting needle was absolutely *useless*) were only too true. But I managed, and really got quite good at coping with a one-handed life. Still, it was with considerable relief that I went back to Casualty when the fortnight was up.

I'm a member of the Hospital Friends Committee and know most of the staff at the hospital, so Sandra Bradshaw, the Sister on duty, greeted me with the easy familiarity of an old acquaintance.

"Well, Sheila, what have you been up to? That plaster looks a bit the worse for wear!"

"I know," I said guiltily. "I knocked over a tin of soup and it went everywhere. I did try to clean this wretched thing, but I only made it worse!"

"Tomato?"

"Carrot and coriander."

"Very colorful, anyway. Right, then." She produced a pair of shears and I shut my eyes while she cut the plaster away.

"Goodness, that's better," I said. "Just to feel the air on my arm again!"

"Don't get too excited — we've got to see how it's mending. I'll send you into X-ray and then Mr. Wheeler can see how it's getting on."

While I was waiting my turn in the X-ray department I thought how lucky we were to have such a good hospital in Taviscombe. It's a cottage hospital, which means that our local G.P.s take turns to be the doctors on duty, but we also have clinics on certain days taken by specialists from the main Taunton hospital. Best of both worlds, really. An old-fashioned way to run a hospital — perhaps that's why it works so well. And because of most of us, staff and patients, having lived in Taviscombe all our lives, there's a sort of family atmosphere that you don't get in big-city hospitals.

Someone came and sat down beside me. It was Susan Campbell, Alan Johnson's sister.

"Hello," I said. "Are you all right? What's the matter?"

"Oh, my knee's been giving me a lot of trouble, so they're going to see if there's anything wrong or if it's just arthritis."

"I'm so sorry. I thought I hadn't seen you about for a while."

"Well, it wasn't just that. Alan's been quite ill and I haven't been able to get about much anyway. He's still pretty bad. Fiona's with him today while I'm out — I don't like to leave him alone."

Fiona is Susan's daughter.

"He's very lucky to have you both living with him. I can't imagine how he'd cope otherwise."

"That's really why we came back from Montreal when Mary died," Susan said. "I didn't like to think of him trying to cope all alone."

"I think it was very noble of you to give up your life there."

"Oh, it wasn't a big deal. I had thought of coming back when Jim, my husband, died, but Fiona was still a teenager and I didn't want to upset her schooling, so we just stayed. But I've always wanted to come back to Taviscombe."

"Well, give Alan my kind regards," I said as I got up to take my turn.

I was sitting on yet another bench, clutching the envelope containing my X-ray, when Dr. Macdonald, my own G.P., came by. He greeted me absently and I thought he looked unusually upset and worried. He went into the office next to where I was sitting, and was joined soon after by Dr.

13

Howard, one of the members of Taviscombe's other group practice. There was a low murmur of conversation, but then I heard Alec Macdonald's voice rising and saying, "It's quite impossible! I've spoken to him about it very strongly and told him that it's absolutely the *last* thing the practice needs just now. . . ." His voice dropped again and as I was straining to hear more, Sandra came and called me in to see Mr. Wheeler.

He was tall and thin, with surprisingly fashionable spiky hair *en brosse*. Like all figures in authority (not just policemen) he seemed, to my elderly eye, very young. However, he dealt most competently with my wrist.

"It will take a little while to mend completely," he said. "I know it's the last thing you want to hear, but your age is against you, I'm afraid. Still, you should regain the full use of it. You must just be patient."

"I haven't got to have another horrible plaster on it, have I?"

He smiled. "No, I think we can get away with just strapping it up, but you must promise to rest it and keep it in the sling as much as possible."

"Oh, yes," I said fervently, "I promise."

Sandra gave me another appointment for three weeks' time and I was on my way out when I saw Alec Macdonald again, on his way to visit the general ward. He was going up the stairs slowly as if it was difficult for him to make any sort of effort, most unlike his usual brisk and lively progress, and I wondered what it was that had upset him so much. Outside, the early-summer day was lovely, and rejoicing in my freedom from the itchy plaster cast, I ran into Rosemary, who insisted that we should go to the Buttery for coffee ("and a nice sugary bun") to celebrate.

"Well, you look better than when I saw you last," she said when we were settled in a quiet corner. "I see you've got the plaster off."

"Such a relief. Not that I can do much more because it's all strapped up and Sandra — you remember Sandra Bradshaw, Molly's daughter; she's a Sister there now — made me promise faithfully not to use it much. Still, the bliss of no itching!"

"Well, do be careful — you don't want to set yourself back. What's this Wheeler person like? Roger came across him in some case or other and said he was very competent."

Roger is Rosemary's son-in-law and a chief inspector in CID.

"He's certainly that. Nice, I thought,

15

though he looks a bit trendy — hair spiked up a bit with gel, which looked odd with a suit."

"Good heavens, what is the medical profession coming to!"

"I saw Alec Macdonald while I was waiting. Now, he really looked his age — he was obviously upset about something and seemed as if he had the weight of the world on his shoulders."

"Well, he is the senior partner of that practice and that must be pretty stressful. Besides, he's getting on a bit — I should think he'll be retiring soon."

"Oh, dear, I hope not. He's been our doctor for ages. I'd hate to have to get used to someone else."

"Jilly says that Joanna Stevenson is very nice."

"I suppose there's a lot to be said for a female doctor. At least they have some idea of what one is going through."

"Though I gather *she* seemed a bit upset last week when Jilly took Delia in about that poisoned finger she has. Anyhow, Jilly said that although Dr. Stevenson was perfectly good with Delia — she's finally put her on to an antibiotic — she was very distrait and not her usual self. I wonder what's going on there."

"Oh, well, if there's any sort of scandal, it'll turn up on the front page of the *Free Press*."

"Which reminds me," Rosemary said, "did you see that article last week about the new traffic system at the bottom of West Street? It's really dreadful."

"I know," I agreed. "There's going to be a bad accident there. Just painting white lines in the road like that — nobody knows who has right of way. And as for the poor pedestrians! I nearly got mown down the other day by a car turning left without indicating."

"It's bad enough for the locals, who know it's a death trap, but all the visitors just drive blithely on not knowing *what* they're supposed to do. And it'll get worse as the season goes on."

Taviscombe was beginning to fill up with summer visitors. The amusement arcades on the seafront opened up, boards advertising ALL-DAY BREAKFASTS and CREAM TEAS appeared outside the cafés, and racks of cheap clothing from the shops in the Avenue obstructed the pavements. There were fewer places to park the car along the seafront, and because of the summer council regulations, I could no longer walk Tris on the beach. Like most residents, I regard the summer invasion

17

with dismay, irritable at the crowded pavements, the longer queues at the supermarket checkouts, the general feeling that the town has been taken over by strangers. But then, I would feel mean at wanting to deny everyone those delights of our coast and hills that we residents so often take for granted.

This day, however, the crossness predominated when I went into Woolworths to get some shoe polish and found the place full of dawdling holidaymakers and overexcited children (who should surely have been in school) blocking the aisles when I was in a hurry. I'd come to a halt in the garden section when I heard a voice behind me.

"I don't know why it is, but it seems to me that the holiday season seems to start earlier every year." I turned and found Alec Macdonald standing behind me, awkwardly burdened by a brightly packaged flowering cherry tree. "How are you, Sheila?" he went on. "I saw you in Casualty — sorry I didn't have time to say hello properly." He indicated the sling that I was dutifully wearing. "What's all this?"

I told him about my fractured wrist and said I'd just been in to have the plaster off and to see Mr. Wheeler.

"Oh, Wheeler's a good man. He'll see you all right."

"He seemed very nice. I've got to see him again in three weeks' time."

"Splendid. You'll be fine."

He nodded benevolently and made his way through the throng towards the door. He seemed to be his normal cheerful self again, so presumably whatever had been upsetting him had been resolved. As Rosemary had said, being the head of a large practice was a stressful business. I found my shoe polish and on my way out I passed the videos and couldn't resist browsing through the children's section to see if there was something suitable to take with me when I went to have supper with Michael and Thea.

"I don't think she's got this Teletubbies one, has she?" I asked when I arrived.

"Alice," Thea called, "come and see what Gran has brought you."

A small sturdy figure came hurtling into the room and hugged me round the knees.

"Alice, careful!" Thea admonished. "Mind poor Gran's wrist."

"She's fine," I said, embracing my granddaughter with one arm. "Aren't you, my love?"

"Present," Alice said, going straight to the point as small children do.

The video was a success, though the grown-ups felt that seeing it twice through was quite enough. Alice reluctantly went up for her bath on the understanding that I would come and read to her ("*How* did the cow jump over the moon, Gran?" "What's a cockleshell?"), so that by the time we all sat down to supper I was quite tired.

"So, how did you get on at the hospital?" Thea asked as she spooned out a generous helping of fish pie. "I thought I'd do something soft that you could eat one-handed."

"Mm, it's lovely," I said. "The smoked haddock makes all the difference. It was wonderful to get the plaster off. The strapping's a bit uncomfortable, but at least it doesn't itch!"

"Well, you be careful," Michael said severely. "Don't go mad."

"As if I would."

"I know for a fact," he continued, "that you've got all those plug plants that need potting on. Now, promise me that you'll leave them till the weekend and I'll come round and do them for you."

"There's no need, really. I can do them a few at a time. . . ."

"No!"

"Well, if you're sure. You both have such busy lives and I really must do what I can."

"I tell you what you can do," Thea said. "You can come with me to the open morning at Alice's nursery school. It's on Friday."

"Oh, yes, I'd love to. Goodness, though, isn't it terrifying how time flies? Nursery school already — it'll be proper school next."

"Then university," Michael said, "then a job, then marriage — should I start saving up for the wedding now? I believe it costs a fortune."

I laughed. "All right, I know I'm being silly, but time does whiz by. Rosemary was only saying this morning that Dr. Macdonald's going to retire next year."

"Well, he must be getting on," Michael said.

"I suppose he must be," I said sadly, "but I still think of him as the young man who took over the practice from old Dr. Milner. Oh, well, we're all getting old."

"You can't get old," Michael said. "With all you've got to do, there simply won't be time."

Chapter Two

"Have you heard about Kenneth Webster?"

I was reluctantly spooning instant coffee into a trayful of cups under Anthea's watchful eye. I usually manage to avoid the weekly coffee mornings at Brunswick Lodge, but Anthea had said it was an emergency. ("Marjorie Read's daughter's had her baby early so she's had to go up to Leamington to look after the twins. I tried everyone else — you were the last resort." Anthea is not known for her diplomacy.)

"No, what about him?"

"In hospital in Taunton," Anthea said. "Taken in as an emergency last Friday. Moira is very upset."

"How awful. What is it?"

"Heart attack. He's in intensive care. It's touch and go."

"Oh, dear, how dreadful. I'd no idea he'd been ill."

"Nor had he," Anthea said, filling up a milk jug from the bottle. "He'd had these pains for a long time and they said it was just mild angina, and then he collapsed just like that."

"But surely —"

"You'd think so, wouldn't you? But no, Dr. Morrison would have it that it wasn't anything serious, and now look what's happened."

"That's terrible!"

"Mind you, I've never liked Dr. Morrison. I had to see him once when Dr. Macdonald was away and I thought he was downright rude. Refused to give me an antibiotic for my bad flu and gave me the most impertinent lecture about bacteria and viruses — some such nonsense, I didn't take in half of it. I'm not in the least surprised he got it wrong in poor Kenneth's case!"

"I wonder if that's why Dr. Macdonald was looking so worried," I said.

"Worried?"

"Yes, I saw him at the hospital when I went to have my plaster off."

"He might well be worried with mistakes like that being made in his practice," Anthea said severely. "That's what happens when you have these group practices. Now, when I used to go to Dr. Milner, things were quite different. A proper family doctor, someone with a real sense of vocation, not like these young things off on *courses* whenever you want them!" She poured sugar into a bowl and got out a collection of teaspoons. "Now then, Sheila, we'll have those cups over there by the urn. Oh, no, of course, you can't manage the tray with that wrist, can you? I'll do it. You just bring the spoons — I imagine you can manage that."

"You know Anthea," I said to Rosemary when she rang to see how I was. "She made me feel that having a fractured wrist was all my fault — though I suppose it was, if you come to think of it — but done on purpose to make life difficult for her."

Rosemary laughed. "She doesn't mean it — well, you know that — she's a kind-hearted soul, she'd do anything for you, but I do agree that she can be maddening! But poor old Ken Webster, though, what a dreadful thing to have happened!"

"It does seem a bit off. I mean, if he's been complaining of pains for some time, then I would have thought that Dr. Morrison might have done *something* about it."

"I believe angina's bit tricky," Rosemary said. "Jack's Uncle Gerald had it for ages and then went, just like that."

"I suppose. I just hope poor Ken's all right — it would be pretty awkward for Dr. Morrison if he died."

"I've never seen him — as a doctor I mean. What's he like?"

"I only saw him once," I said, "about a year ago, when I had a chest infection. He seemed all right. A bit morose, I thought, definitely not chatty."

"Morose isn't really what you want in a doctor," Rosemary said thoughtfully. "Chat does ease things along somehow."

"And he was very uncooperative about an X-ray, now I come to think of it," I said. "I felt he was counting the pennies in a rather grudging way. I mean, I know they've got to work to a budget, but he seemed to me to be carrying things a bit far! Anyway, I think he's the sort of person who thinks he's always right — a bit arrogant and sure of himself."

"Perhaps that's what happened with Ken."

"I wouldn't be surprised. That's probably why he put off consulting someone else until it was too late. Well, certainly Anthea doesn't think much of him. She was very scathing. Oh, yes, that reminds me, she asked if I'd put my name down for the theater party to Bath that she's organizing. Are you going?"

"I'd have loved to, but Jilly has to take Delia to the dentist that day and I promised

I'd fetch Alex from school," said Rosemary. "Are you going?"

"I wasn't sure — I seem to have seen *The Seagull* so many times, but it *is* a pre-London production and it is Sonia Marshall and she's always worth seeing. Anyway, I didn't really have a choice. Anthea said they needed some more people to fill the coach so that was that!"

"I expect you'll enjoy it," Rosemary said. "And it's always nice to go to Bath."

I arrived at the coach stop rather late (having tried, unsuccessfully, to get Foss in before I left) and the only remaining seat was the one next to Anthea, who spent the journey complaining about the difficulties of organizing *anything* (with special emphasis on the problems of block booking for a matinee and the vagaries of the coach company) and vowing she would never take on such a thankless task again. Since this was standard procedure for such occasions, I let it all flow over me; I simply said "How awful" and "Poor you" at intervals and occupied the journey with my own thoughts and anticipation of the treat to come.

I do love what I always think of as a proper theater. Modern provincial theaters are splendid and give those of us who live outside the big cities a chance to see some sort of dramatic entertainment. But I do miss the plush, the gilt and the brilliance of the chandeliers — the atmosphere, in effect, of an old theater. The Theatre Royal in Bath is so full of history that you feel it would be quite natural for the curtain to rise on Kean's Othello or Mrs. Siddons's Lady Macbeth. In the old days Peter and I used to have what we called Theater Week, when we'd have a glorious splurge and spend a whole week in London, going to a matinee and an evening performance every day. We ended up with a sort of cultural indigestion, but it was wonderful, and now that I get up to London so rarely — and even then for more mundane reasons than theatergoing — I do miss the sheer pleasure of just *being* there and watching the curtain (provincial theaters often don't have a curtain) slowly rising, a thrill that takes me back to those magic moments in my childhood when I could hardly breathe for excitement.

It was a really good production and we all reassembled in the coach feeling well pleased with our day. Determined to avoid a return journey with Anthea, I made my way to the back of the coach and found a seat next to Susan Campbell's daughter, Fiona.

"Hello," I said, "do you mind if I sit with you?"

"Please do," she said. "Would you rather sit by the window?"

"No, this is fine. Did you enjoy the play?"

"Oh, yes. Sonia Marshall was wonderful — I've only ever seen her on television before — that hat she wore, fantastic! And I thought the end where the girl comes back was very well-done and where the young man shoots himself, that was very sad."

"Yes," I said, slightly taken aback by this rather prosaic appreciation of Chekhov's masterpiece. "It was, wasn't it? I was so pleased to see you here," I went on. "I'm sure you deserve a treat after all your splendid work in looking after poor Alan. How is he?"

"It's good news," Fiona said. "Dr. Morrison referred him to a consultant and they're going to do a bypass. They reckon that will make a lot of difference."

"I'm sure it will," I said warmly. "I've known several people who've had it done and it's completely transformed their lives. When are they going to do it?"

"Quite soon, he's having it done privately in Bristol."

"Well, I do hope all goes well. It should make life easier for you and your mother.

How is she, by the way? I saw her in X-ray last week. A problem with her knee, I think she said."

"Oh, that's all right — it was just a pulled ligament. She's a bit tired and run-down."

"Not surprising! Well, let me know how the operation goes."

"Perhaps you'd come and see him when he gets home — he always likes to see visitors."

"Of course. I'd like that."

"Well," Rosemary said, "Dr. Morrison's obviously taken fright after what happened to Ken — and that was really terrible; poor Moira's absolutely distraught — so he isn't taking any chances with Alan."

"What's happened to Ken?"

"Haven't you heard? He died two days ago."

"No!"

"Another massive heart attack."

"How dreadful. Awful for Moira. And for their son."

"Richard? Yes, he came down from London when Ken first went into hospital. He's in a terrible state — talking about suing the practice, that sort of thing."

"Oh, dear. That will upset Moira even more."

"I'm afraid so. And of course, it might

have happened anyway — I think they'd have a job to prove negligence."

"Still," I said, "they'll always say it was Dr. Morrison's fault, no matter what, and I must say I don't really blame them. I wonder how he's feeling now?"

As it happened I saw him a few days later. I was in the surgery waiting to arrange for a new prescription when he came through on his way out — a tall man, though slightly built, really rather good-looking if you like that dark, saturnine type, in his early forties, I suppose, though he could be any age. He strode through the waiting room, looking straight ahead, ignoring the dozen people sitting there, where the other doctors would have acknowledged their presence with a smile or a nod.

"He's a funny sort of man," said a voice behind me in the queue at the reception desk. It was Mrs. Fielding, an elderly woman I knew slightly from Brunswick Lodge. "I wouldn't fancy him as my doctor. That Dr. Morrison, the one who's just gone out. You hear all sorts of things about him."

"Really?"

"Thinks a lot of himself, won't ever admit he might be wrong. They say he's lost several patients through that."

I saw that the rumors were already flying about and I was just about to ask what she'd heard, when it was my turn at reception, so I had to turn away.

Alan Johnson had his operation and when he was back home again, Susan rang me and asked if I'd go and see him.

"I wonder if you'd mind coming tomorrow afternoon?" she asked. "Only I've got an appointment to have my eyes tested and Fiona's at work and I'd feel better if someone could be here."

"No, that's fine," I said. "What time?"

"Oh, that is good of you. Would about half past three be all right?"

When I arrived she greeted me warmly. "Thank you so much for coming. He's been really looking forward to seeing you. He gets very fed up just sitting about watching TV and it'll do him a world of good to see an old friend."

Susan was already wearing her coat.

"Forgive me if I dash off straightaway, won't you?" she said. "Only I'd like to do a bit of shopping before my appointment. I've only just made the tea and I've left it all ready in the sitting room, if you wouldn't mind helping yourself. . . ."

I found Alan sitting in front of the television watching a garden makeover program.

"No, don't try to get up," I said as he cast aside the rug over his knees and made as if to rise. "How are you?"

"Better, I suppose," he said grudgingly. "No, that's not fair — I'm much better — just that I get bored hanging about the house like this watching rubbishy television programs. I ask you — fancy covering your garden with gravel and planks of wood — *decking*." He pronounced the word with loathing. "What's wrong with a nice bit of grass? That's what I'd like to know!"

I laughed. "Oh, I do agree. I can't bear to think how many creepy-crawlies might be living under all that wood! Never mind, you'll soon be out and about. You're looking so much better."

"Yes, well," he said, reluctant quite to relinquish his invalid state. "I've a way to go yet, but they're pleased with how the operation went."

"It's a pity you couldn't have had it before."

"Dr. Morrison said it was the last resort. He wanted to try medication first."

"Still . . ."

"I know some people don't like him, but I've always got on well with him. Doesn't say much, but he knows what he's doing. He

32

explained a lot about heart conditions. Of course, there's always been that problem in my family. I told him, my father and his brother both died of heart trouble and then there's Susan."

"Susan?"

"Yes, she's had a problem for years — she had to have a pacemaker fitted when she was in Canada."

"Really? I never knew that."

"Well, you know Susan, not one to make a fuss. Anyway, Dr. Morrison was very interested — he's doing some sort of research for a pharmaceutical company about genes and hereditary illnesses or something."

"I didn't know that."

"Oh, yes. That's why it's more difficult to get an appointment to see him. He's only in two days a week."

"That's not very satisfactory, surely."

"Oh, a lot of them are doing it now — I suppose it's all extra money. Mind you, I think some of the other doctors in the practice are a bit annoyed about it."

"I'm not surprised, if it's all extra work for them."

"I suppose so, or else they're jealous that they didn't get in there first!"

I laughed. "It could be that. Now then, shall I pour the tea?"

Susan had laid out the tea things on one of the small Oriental tables that were scattered about the room. In his young days Alan had worked as an engineer in India and the Middle East.

"Such a pretty table," I said as I put milk into the cups and cut slices of the ginger cake that Susan had left. "You have some lovely things."

"Yes, some of the high-ups in the Gulf were always giving us presents — quite embarrassing sometimes. I remember, one of our chaps was presented with a couple of hawks — it was considered a tremendous compliment and a deadly insult to refuse. Poor Trevor had an awful job getting out of that one! I came back with all that lot," he said, indicating a cabinet full of gilt bowls and various other objects richly decorated and enameled. "I had to get a cabinet to put them in. Poor Mary got fed up with dusting them and Susan has never really liked them — too showy, she says!"

"They are rather exotic," I said, getting up to examine them more closely, "but very beautiful. Do you miss that life?"

He thought for a moment. "Not really," he said. "Certainly not now. It's a young man's life. No, give me good old England any day."

"I gather Susan feels the same, or do you think she misses Montreal?"

"I don't think so. She doesn't talk about it much. Nowadays we talk a lot about the old days, when we were children and things like that."

"I suppose we all do that as we get older," I agreed, handing him his tea.

"It's been very good the way she's settled back here, and Fiona too. She's a lovely girl, more like a daughter to me than a niece. Poor Mary would have loved her — it was always a sadness to her that we never had children of our own."

"Fiona seems very happy in her job," I said.

"Took to it like a duck to water. I knew that George Lewis — he's my solicitor — was looking for someone for the office and Fiona is marvelous with computers and things like that. Anyway, she's fitted in wonderfully well there and they want her to train as a legal exec."

"That's splendid."

"Yes, we've got a lot to be thankful for — especially me. Do you know, I think I could manage another piece of that cake."

Chapter Three

"You must be really glad to have that strapping off," Thea said, folding a pair of small bright red dungarees and putting them in the laundry basket. "You know, she's almost out of these and I only bought them for her a few months ago."

"They grow in bursts," I said. "They go along just the same size for ages and then suddenly they've grown out of everything all at once — it happens, especially with shoes, just you wait."

"Oh, don't. That's started already — how I wish she could have stayed in knitted bootees forever!"

I laughed. "Still, it's such fun buying clothes for little girls. Little boys' clothes are so boring — all they want are camouflage trousers and jackets."

"Girls wear those too — though fortunately not at Alice's age. But about the wrist," Thea continued, "how is it?"

"Oh, much better," I said, "thank goodness. It's still not very strong. I've got to have physio and do exercises and things."

"Will you go to Jean?"

"Oh, yes, she's very good." Jean is Anthea's elder daughter and used to be head of the physio department at the hospital, but she's recently set up on her own. "And even if she wasn't, I'd never hear the last of it from Anthea if I went to someone else."

Our medical practice — or I suppose I ought to call it a medical complex — is housed in a purpose-built collection of buildings. The general-practice side is arranged round a courtyard with corridors on all four sides and a general entrance that is shared with the other, alternative-medicine section — all very modern and holistic in concept and in practice. Jean and her physiotherapy is on the alternative side along with the reflexologists, homeopaths, chiropractors, aromatherapists, hypnotherapists and all the other (to me) exotic practitioners.

Jean is a nice girl, cheerful and friendly, only a hint of her mother's domineering nature evident in her brisk and professional manner.

"Hello, Sheila, I heard from Mother about your fall. A hairline fracture of the radius, wasn't it?"

"Yes, that's right."

While she was working on the wrist she kept up a flow of easy chat, about Michael and Thea and Alice, about her husband, Roy, and her two boys, and about her sister, Kathy — now married to Ben Turner, one of our vets, and expecting a baby in the autumn.

"Joanna Stevenson's expecting a baby too," she said.

"Really?"

"Yes, they're a bit fed up about it next door." She nodded in the direction of the G.P.s' section. "They're very short-staffed as it is, what with Dr. Morrison and Dr. Porter only coming in part-time. There's Dr. Macdonald, of course, and Joanna's husband, Clive Stevenson, but they'll still be pretty stretched."

"Still it's nice for the Stevensons. Is it their first?"

"Yes, and Joanna's coming back to the practice after the baby's born."

"So many mothers do now."

"Economic necessity," Jean said. "And, of course, if you've had a long and expensive training, you don't feel like giving it all up. I know that's how I felt."

"I'm sure that's true."

"Thea doesn't regret giving up the law?" Jean asked.

"Oh, no. It was never her choice anyway — she only did it to please her father. No, she seems quite happy being at home with Alice."

"Perhaps she'll go back when Alice is older."

"Perhaps."

"Joanna's really keen to get back," Jean said. "Can you move your wrist a little bit, towards me if you can — that's fine. I think her career means a lot to her, but I don't think Clive is too happy about it. I think he hoped she might want to stay at home and look after the baby."

"Really?"

"Well, actually I think they've found it difficult working together in the same practice."

"Oh?"

"They're both quite competitive and I imagine they're both the sort who take their work home with them, as the saying goes."

"It must be difficult."

"Oh, it's *all* difficult," Jean said, sighing, "and trying to balance work and children is sometimes quite impossible. I just hope Joanna realizes it! Mind you, it's easier for me now that both the boys are in their teens, and Roy is marvelous, but even so, I'm always tired nowadays." She laughed. "Perhaps Thea is the one who's got it right."

She removed the pads from my wrist and switched off her machine.

"That feels much better," I said gratefully.

"Good. Now I'm going to show you some exercises and you must promise me faithfully to do them regularly every day."

"It is rather a bore," I said to Rosemary, moving my wrist in the manner Jean had prescribed, "but I suppose if it's going to make it better, I must do them."

"Of course you must," Rosemary said firmly. "Get the strength back."

"I know," I said resentfully. "At *our* age everything takes that much longer — I wish they wouldn't all keep saying that. I know it's true, but I don't want to hear it. There, now," I said, "that's the lot. Now we can have a nice cup of coffee. I must say it's a real pleasure to be able to open the biscuit tin again without help."

"Did you say that Joanna Stevenson was having a baby?" Rosemary asked.

"So Jean said."

"So she'll be off for several months, then."

"Yes, I suppose they'll have to get someone in to cover for her — I mean, they're pretty stretched now."

"That's true. It's getting really difficult to make an appointment."

"Anyway," I said, "locums aren't very satisfactory however good they may be as doctors."

"Jilly will be upset," Rosemary said. "She says Joanna Stevenson is really good with the children. I hope she won't leave when she's had the baby."

"Jean doesn't think that's very likely, though apparently Clive Stevenson would be glad if she did." I told her what Jean had told me. "I suppose there could be friction if they're both working in the same practice."

"I suspect it's because she's a better doctor than he is and he knows it and resents it," Rosemary said. "I've only seen him a couple of times, when Dr. Macdonald was away, and it never seemed to me that he had any confidence in himself. You know, he was always a bit tentative — might be this, might be that."

"A lot of them are like that now," I said, pouring us both more coffee, "off-loading their patients onto a specialist at the first sign of trouble."

"Not the first sign," Rosemary said, "think of poor Ken Webster!"

"Yes, that will make them all more cautious than ever. Though, actually, with Dr.

Morrison it's arrogance more than lack of confidence — always sure that he's right and everyone else is wrong. Goodness, how one longs for the *certainty* of dear old Dr. Milner — I suppose he didn't always get it right, but at least you knew where you were with him!"

"Well, you know where you are with Clive Stevenson," Rosemary said, "and it's not where you want to be! I must say," she went on, "I can't imagine what Joanna saw in him. I mean, she's very attractive, pretty, clever and efficient, and he's such a — such a nonperson!"

"Oh, well, who knows what anyone sees in anyone?" I said. "Look at Angela and Paul Lyall — he's brilliant and gorgeous and she's a little mouse of a thing, but they've been married for over thirty years and seem perfectly happy."

Because it's a bit heavy, Thea very kindly left my ironing board set up in what I still think of as Michael's room so that I could do some ironing when the spirit moved me. I rather like ironing, especially if I have the radio on. It's a pleasant mindless occupation and you do have something to show for it when it's done. As I moved the iron slowly over one of the kitchen curtains I considered what Rosemary and I had been saying about our medical center and the doctors in it. Of course we're grateful for all the new, miraculous treatments that keep us alive when we might otherwise be dead, and I do see that with an amazing number of patients to look after (how many thousands in each practice — it seems incredible) they can't spare more than ten minutes for each patient. A group medical center is the only way to go now — I quite understood that — but I, and most of my generation, can't help being nostalgic for the days of the single-doctor practice. The days of the family doctor, in fact, when treatment was on a personal level and the doctor would "just pop in to see how you are," sometimes at inconvenient times (Dr. Milner was a great one for calling before breakfast), but always in touch.

"Oh, well," I said to Foss, who, drawn by the prospect of some sort of entertainment, had followed me upstairs and was at present sitting comfortably on the warm pile of newly ironed garments, "I suppose I'm just another silly old woman who wants things back the way they were. Though goodness knows there are a lot of things I wouldn't want back."

Radio 3, which had been filling the room

with the gentle sound of Delius, suddenly embarked on some loud atonal modern music, which caused Foss to leap off the bed, scattering the pile of garments. With a sigh, I folded my curtains, switched off the radio and the iron, and prepared to go and get some lunch.

"Jean said you'd been in to see her," Anthea said when I ran into her outside the post office. "She said she's given you some exercises to do."

Anthea likes to keep au fait with the movements of all her friends and, indeed, mere acquaintances.

"Yes, she was very helpful."

"I hope you're doing them regularly — that's the important thing."

"Oh, yes," I said, thinking of the times when I'd forgotten or just couldn't be bothered. Still, as the wrist seemed to be getting better of its own accord, I didn't feel too guilty. "Jean is really splendid," I went on hastily before Anthea could cross-question me further, "and I gather that she's got quite a lot of patients now."

"Most encouraging. Really more than she can cope with sometimes. She may have to get an assistant and that isn't always a good thing."

"I suppose being part of the medical center helps," I said.

"A mixed blessing," Anthea said severely.

"Really?"

"The place is not run the way I would like it."

That didn't surprise me, since Anthea's views on any organization tend to be critical.

"In what way?" I asked.

"Well, some of these alternative-medicine people" — she pronounced the words with distaste — "seem to have some very weird ideas. Massaging people's *feet*," she said, "and expecting that to cure, well, all sorts of things. And rubbing scent all over them — whatever next!"

"A lot of people believe in it," I said.

"I'm not sure it's good for Jean to be mixed up with things like that."

"The Prince of Wales is very keen on alternative medicine," I said. Anthea is a fervent royalist.

"So they *say*, but I for one don't believe everything I read in the papers."

"Well," I said hastily, trying to get Anthea off one of her many hobbyhorses, "I'm glad that Jean's doing so well. It's always something of a risk setting up on your own."

"Oh, Jean is very levelheaded. She had it all worked out before she made any decision."

"I'm sure she would have. She's always been a very practical girl. And then of course, she's very handy for the general-practice side of the center — I expect she gets a lot of referrals from the doctors."

"Quite a few, though most of her patients come privately, which is much more satisfactory for Jean — all those dreadful forms for the NHS."

"Dr. Macdonald always speaks very highly of her."

"Oh, well, Dr. Macdonald, he's a proper doctor, one of the old school, not like some of the others."

"Oh, I don't know. . . ."

"Well, we all know about Dr. Morrison — poor Ken Webster. And as for making appointments, take this new system they've got." Anthea settled more comfortably in a space out of the way of the other post office users and prepared to hold forth, while I resignedly put my heavy shopping bag down and prepared to listen. "All this nonsense about not booking appointments in advance and having to ring up on the morning you want to see anyone. Everyone ringing at the same time, the line's always engaged, and then when you *do* get through, all the appointments you can manage have gone!"

"I know," I said with feeling, "it's absolutely maddening. I can't think what was wrong with the old system — it always seemed to work quite well."

"Some of those receptionists are power mad!" Anthea declared.

"Oh, not Valerie Carter," I protested, "she's a nice little thing and always tries to be helpful."

"She's all right," Anthea admitted grudgingly, "but that Lorna Spear, she's dreadful. Of course, she's Janet Dobson's daughter — do you remember what a disagreeable girl she was? — and then this Lorna married Ronald Spear, a shifty sort of man if ever I saw one. I wasn't at all surprised when he ran off with that girl from the florist."

"Lorna can be a bit abrasive at times," I said.

"Abrasive! Downright rude, I call it. The other day, when she finally admitted that I could make an appointment with Dr. Macdonald an exact — *exact,* mind you — week ahead, she said that I couldn't this time because he'd be away on a course. Really triumphant, she sounded. I just put the phone down!"

"I know. Sometimes I just give up and

make an appointment with Nancy." Nancy Williams is our nurse-practitioner and absolutely brilliant. In fact an awful lot of people choose to go to her rather than one of the doctors, not just because it's less hassle, but because she gives her patients the individual attention we all crave.

"Yes, Nancy's very good — oh, there's Maureen. I must go — I want a word with her about the next coffee morning."

"But Anthea's right," I said to Thea, "it is getting impossible."

"I know. Do you remember, we had to take Alice down to Casualty when she had that bad ear infection a while back and we couldn't get to see any of the doctors?"

"Yes, I remember. Thank goodness they're all so brilliant in Casualty. We're very lucky to have them."

"Oh, I agree, but still, we shouldn't have to rely on them."

"Have you decided what to do about Alice's vaccinations," I asked, "all this MMR business?"

"Well, she had German measles when she was very young and mumps isn't so important for a girl, so what I'd really like to do is just have her done for measles if I can."

"I must say I agree with you. I know they

say it's quite safe and I'm sure it is, but — well, if there's even the faintest, *minuscule* chance, I wouldn't want to risk it. What does Michael say?" I asked.

"Much the same. So I think that's what we'll do."

"Oh, good. It's all getting a bit much — everyone is so bombarded with medical information these days — all those articles in magazines and newspapers, you really don't know what to believe. And then there's all this stuff about marvelous new treatments."

"People's expectations are so much higher now, without enough doctors to cope with the demand," Thea said, pouring some milk into a mug. "Alice, leave your drawing, darling, and come and have your milk."

Alice, who had been sitting at the kitchen table laboriously engaged in some sort of artwork that required many different felt-tip pens, picked up the drawing and brought it over. It featured two brown circles with two green circles inside the smaller one and two triangles on the top. What appeared to be a brown snake was wrapped around the whole.

"That's lovely, darling," Thea said. "I'll put it up on the fridge."

"No," Alice said firmly, removing it from her mother's grasp. "It's for Gran. Picture of

Smoke for Gran." She went over to where Smoke was sleeping and gently laid her face against the cat's soft fur.

"Oh, thank you, darling," I said. "It's beautiful and just like her. I'll take it home and put it on my fridge so that Tris and Foss can see it as well."

Chapter Four

I was standing by the kitchen window watching a raven hoovering up the bread I'd put out on the lawn. He was a majestic bird with a great air of authority, so that even the magpies, usually so full of themselves, stood back respectfully. When the phone rang and I moved to answer it, the raven, sensing the movement, rose slowly in the air (his dignity no whit impaired by the large crusts of bread sticking out from his formidable beak) and flapped away, leaving the remaining morsels for the lesser creatures.

"Sheila?" It was Susan Campbell. "Sorry to ring you so early, but we're having a small drinks party on the fifteenth for Alan's birthday and I want to get the numbers fixed. It's his seventieth so I thought we must do something to celebrate. He's much better now, so I don't think it'll be too much for him."

"What a nice idea, I'd love to come."

"He seems quite keen. I was going to keep

it as a surprise, but then I thought that with a heart condition the last thing you want are surprises!"

"Very true! What sort of time?"

"About six thirty to eight thirty — the usual — I'm sure he'll be able to manage that long. Actually, he'll be so glad to see everyone again. You know how sociable he is. He goes out for quite long walks and so on — he has to have quite a bit of exercise — but I've tried to keep things fairly low-key otherwise, just to be on the safe side."

"But how about you? You must have had a lot to cope with."

"Oh, I had this wretched cold that got onto my chest and I couldn't seem to shake it off."

"I'm sorry, how miserable for you. You do sound very croaky."

"Alan's been fussing about it so I'm going to see Dr. Morrison sometime. But I'm sure it will clear up soon now that summer really seems to be coming at last — hasn't the weather been wonderful? I do hope it's like this on the fifteenth. Then people can go out into the garden if they want to."

When I'd finished speaking to Susan I went upstairs to get ready for a Hospital Friends Committee meeting. I was looking forward to it rather more than usual because

Dr. Morrison was coming to tell us about some marvelous new apparatus we were being asked to raise funds for and I was glad to have the chance of seeing him in action, as it were. When I arrived, though, he was late and some of the committee members were starting to get restless.

"Nearly twenty minutes," Brian Norris said, looking at his watch. "It's not good enough — I'm a busy man and I've got better things to do with my time than sit about waiting for some doctor to deign to show up."

"Well, he *is* a doctor," Mary Chapman observed acidly, "so perhaps that is *why* he is late. And as for being busy, I imagine Dr. Morrison is much busier than any of us here."

There were murmurs of assent — Brian is not the most popular member of the committee, being overfull of his own importance, and anyone who can take him down a peg usually meets with approval from the other members.

"There might have been an emergency," Maureen Dawson said. "He may be saving someone's life at this very moment."

Since Maureen is known for her passion for drama this comment was rightly ignored.

"Still," Gavin Worsley said, "he might have sent a message if he knew he was running late."

There was general approval of this remark, which was felt to express the view of the majority without the excesses of Brian's outburst. Fortunately, just at this moment Dr. Morrison appeared. He apologized briefly for being late (though without specifying the reason), sat down at the head of the table, opened his briefcase, briskly arranged several papers in front of him and began.

He was certainly a good speaker. He described the equipment, a new sort of digital X-ray machine, clearly and in detail. He told us about its benefits, its price, its cost-effectiveness, its advantages over previous equipment and the research that had gone into it — and all in language everyone could understand.

"I am sure," he concluded, "both the staff and the patients will appreciate its many advantages. As you know, our budget is ridiculously limited, given the number of patients we deal with, especially in the holiday period, and the only way we can secure this important piece of equipment is if it is paid for by voluntary contributions. The Hospital Friends have, in the past, done excellent work in this field and I am sure that this will be the latest in a long line of things you have all done to improve the work of this hospital." He shuffled the papers together. "Any questions?"

Brian, who prided himself on being a shrewd businessman who let nothing get past him, said, "We've already got what we were told is a state-of-the-art X-ray machine — bought with money that the Friends raised for it. Why do we need this new thing?"

Dr. Morrison looked at him coldly. "I have already explained the benefits of this new machine and how much more efficient it is. It is digital and can send images to the hospital in Taunton instantly on request, thus saving time that may well be critical in the treatment of a seriously ill patient. It will, as I have also explained, save money in the long run. Science is always moving forward and I feel it is important that we take advantage of the progress that is being made."

Not surprisingly, after that, no one else had any questions.

"I think we are all grateful to Dr. Morrison," Mary Chapman said smoothly, "for taking the time to come and tell us about this marvelous new machine, and we will certainly do our utmost to try to raise money for it."

Dr. Morrison nodded briefly and got to his feet.

"We usually have a cup of coffee after our meetings," Maureen said. "Won't you join us?"

His refusal was not exactly curt, but it was very plain he had no wish to stay. With another slight nod in our general direction, he picked up his briefcase and left.

"Well, that wasn't very polite," Maureen said. "People always stay for coffee."

Later that afternoon I had an appointment with Jean. She manipulated my wrist a bit and said, "It's coming along quite nicely. I do hope you've been doing those exercises I gave you." I mumbled something that could be taken for assent and she continued. "I think a couple more sessions should be enough, but I'd like you to see Dr. Macdonald sometime soon just to get his opinion."

"Well, I will," I said, "*if* I can get an appointment. It's really difficult and I suppose it'll be even worse when they start going on holiday. I suppose Joanna Stevenson will be off on maternity leave soon and Dr. Porter has youngish children and has to stick to the school holidays. I don't know about Dr. Morrison — does he have a family?"

"Divorced," Jean said briefly, fixing the little pads to my wrist and switching on the machine. "I don't think there were any children, though."

"Where does his ex-wife live?" I asked.

"Oh, London, of course. She was at the same big teaching hospital that he was."

"Really?"

"They were both working on this research team."

"What sort of research, do you know?"

"Something very high-powered about genetics — I don't know the details. Are you still getting the tingling or shall I turn it up a bit?"

"Turn it up a bit, I think. So what on earth is a man like that doing down here in a country practice?"

"I don't really know. They say he was absolutely brilliant in his field, but there was some sort of bad disagreement, I believe — I don't know the details."

"Still, if he was that important, surely he wouldn't just give up and retreat into obscurity, not a man like him."

"It does seem odd, I agree, but then he's an odd sort of man altogether," Jean said.

"He's certainly a bit abrupt. He came to

speak to the Hospital Friends today and his manner was, to put it mildly, dismissive."

"I know what you mean — it's no wonder he's not liked. Well, that's not entirely true. He does seem to appeal to some women. I gather there are a couple of them who are very keen on him."

"Really? Is he into some sort of relationship, then?"

"Nothing permanent, as far as I know, but no one seems to know much about his private life. He lives out at Porlock Weir, one of those houses up on the hill overlooking the sea, quite remote really and very quiet."

"Oh, I have a friend who lives out there, Nora Burton. Your mother would remember her. I wonder if she ever sees him."

Jean detached the little pads and wiped the gel off my wrist. "There we go," she said. "Now, don't forget to have a word with Dr. Macdonald and keep up the exercises and I'll make an appointment for you in about a fortnight's time."

I was pleased to see that Valerie Carter was on the reception desk at the medical practice when I went across to try and make an appointment. I gave her my best friendly smile and said, "Oh, Valerie, is there *any* chance you can make me an appointment to see Dr. Macdonald sometime?"

"He's very booked up, I'm afraid."

"Could you squeeze me in anywhere?"

She fiddled about with the computer for a bit and then said, "Well . . . well, let me see. I think I can do you eleven thirty this time next week. Would that be all right?"

"That's marvelous," I said. "Thank you so much." I got out my diary and put down the date. "How's your father? Has he had his hip operation?"

"Oh, yes, he's fine, thank you, Mrs. Malory. Really good now, it's made all the difference. In fact he and my mother are going to Malta for three weeks at the end of the month."

"That's splendid. It really is a wonderful operation. I know several people who've had it and it's transformed their lives! Do give them both my regards and say I hope they have a lovely holiday."

"The time one has to spend oiling the wheels," I said to Rosemary. "I mean, Valerie's a nice girl and I like her, but if *she* hadn't been on the desk — if it had been Lorna Spear, for example — and if I hadn't known her parents forever, then I might have had to sit there hanging on to the phone one morning trying to get through to make an appointment on the day."

"I know," Rosemary agreed. "It's getting worse. Everyone's got a horror story. It's nobody's fault, I suppose, just not enough doctors to go round — and I expect we notice it more now we're getting on and *need* them more. And it's not just receptionists," she went on. "Shop assistants who can't be bothered to interrupt their conversation to attend to you, repairmen who never come when they say they will, and — oh, all sorts of people. I really do despair of the way things are!"

"I know," I said with feeling. "I was in the bank the other day and the standard of service there was quite appalling —" I broke off and laughed. "Oh, dear, listen to us — change and decay in all that I see!"

"But it's true," Rosemary protested. "Things were better when we were young."

"Perhaps it's because we *were* young," I suggested. "I suppose you always complain about things more when you're getting old — look at your mother!"

Rosemary laughed. "Oh, Mother was born complaining and she's never stopped since. Which reminds me, she was hinting the other day — what do I mean *hinting*? Mother never hints. She was saying that she hasn't seen you for ages."

"Oh, dear, yes, I've been meaning to go

60

round, but what with this" — I indicated my wrist — "it's all been a bit hectic."

"I explained about your wrist," Rosemary said, "but I think that's an added attraction — she can't wait to hear all about it. You know what she's like about accidents or illness of any kind — just like Queen Victoria!"

"I really will go and see her soon," I said. "I've been feeling a bit guilty that it's been so long."

"Mother is very good at making people feel guilty," Rosemary said grimly, "but it would be nice if you could find the time. Several of her friends have died just lately — there aren't that many left now — and I think she's feeling lonely. Of course Jilly and I pop in most days, but we're usually in a rush and on our way to doing other things. It's not like a *visit,* you know, someone sitting down and having tea and making conversation, someone, I suppose, to make an effort for."

"You're probably right. Isn't it funny, though, how different we all are? As *I* get older I want to make less effort and nowadays I try to avoid anything out of my usual routine."

"Oh, I *do* know what you mean," Rosemary said earnestly. "Anything! Even one's nearest and dearest. Much as I want to see them, I always feel exhausted when the family's been round. Not physical exhaustion so much — although Alex is at that noisy age when they can't keep still for five minutes and it does wear you out — but the sheer mental effort of having to talk to a roomful of people."

"Not just people," I said, "though I do agree about that, but taking on new things. I mean, I can just about manage the things I've taken on already. You know, Brunswick Lodge and the Hospital Friends, though those are getting a bit much nowadays. But like a fool I agreed to do a paper for a symposium — well it's a sort of a festschrift really for Margaret Stanford when she retires from her chair at Cambridge."

"What's it about?"

"The whole thing is called 'In Sickness and in Health' and it's about illness in the Victorian novel — I'm supposed to be doing Charlotte M. Yonge."

"It sounds a bit dismal to me," Rosemary said. "It's that Queen Victoria thing again, I suppose — they really did like to wallow!"

"Well, there's certainly a lot of illness in the novels, and quite often one of the characters is the sort of invalid who spends most of the book on a couch being an inspiration or an irritation to everyone else. She was very good at the details — fever, tuberculosis, spinal injuries — one of her female characters even has a foot amputated."

"Goodness! It all sounds absolutely ghastly. I can't imagine why you're so mad about her!"

"I suppose it's because she's a brilliant storyteller — once you've got into the book you can't put it down. And there's not many modern writers you can say *that* about."

After my conversation with Rosemary I felt obliged to get down to work on my paper, though, as always, I kept finding household tasks that simply *had* to be done first. I prepared the vegetables for supper (to save time later), I put out the papers for the salvage collection (they'd be calling the day after tomorrow and I might forget if I left them), I cooked Foss's fish (very important), I washed out some dusters (I found a couple in a drawer that looked a bit grubby), and I had a go at cleaning the grill (before the grease got burned onto it). Finally, when I could find nothing else to do that could conceivably be called urgent, I went into the study and began to get out the books I needed, and sorted out the notes I'd made.

I sat down at my desk, switched on my

computer and looked glumly at what I'd already written. It seemed to me to be trite and boring. Everything that I might want to say on the subject had, it seemed to me, been said by somebody else. I tried to concentrate, flicking through copies of *The Daisy Chain*, *Pillars of the House*, *The Heir of Redclyffe* and *Beechcroft at Rockstone* and, as usual, getting sidetracked into reading compelling but irrelevant passages.

I was sharply disturbed from my studies by a loud crash from the kitchen. I got up and went out to find the large jug I kept on the windowsill, with various cuttings I was trying to root in water, on the floor smashed to pieces. There was water and broken pottery everywhere and carnation and begonia cuttings scattered over the work top and floor. There were also wet paw marks where Tris had been investigating the phenomenon. He was sitting, looking at the chaos with interest, ears cocked, but I knew, of course, that it was not his doing. The culprit, as I could see from the smaller paw marks, had made his escape and was probably already hiding behind the bed in the spare room, from whence he would emerge later with a blandly innocent expression, as if to inquire what all the fuss was about.

With a sigh, I got down on my knees with a cloth and began to restore the kitchen to some semblance of order.

Chapter Five

I was early for my appointment with Dr. Macdonald and my heart sank when I went into the waiting room because it was absolutely full, which meant that they were running late and I'd have to wait even longer. I sat down in one of the few remaining seats and picked up a copy of *Yachting World* (Dr. Porter was keen on sailing and kept a boat in the harbor), which was the only literature on offer. It didn't hold my attention for very long and to avoid looking down at the carpet (why do all doctors' and dentists' waiting rooms have busy patterned carpets that make you dizzy to look at them?) I looked around me. As I said, the place was full and there were three receptionists in the far section, behind their glass pane — Lorna Spear, my little friend Valerie, and Judith Taylor, whom I didn't know very well because she's been with the practice for only a couple of months. Lorna was on duty at the desk and the other two were drinking coffee with Joanna Stevenson, who'd come through from the corridor that led to the consulting rooms.

From time to time Nancy Williams, the nurse-practitioner, or one of the two nurses came through the door at the near end of the waiting room and called someone in. They seemed to be getting through their lists quicker than the doctors, since Dr. Macdonald and Dr. Morrison (they seemed to be the two doctors on duty) appeared only occasionally to summon a patient. Most of the people, as I looked round, seemed to be sunk in a sort of lethargy, a suspended animation, except for an elderly couple who were engaged in a low-toned conversation — at least, she was delivering a monologue and he was nodding from time to time but obviously not listening. In the corner where the children's toys were set out, a young mother was rocking a pushchair, trying to quieten a fractious toddler, while an older child played with the toys, making occasional forays into the rest of the room, under the feet of the grown-ups. I turned back to *Yachting World* in an attempt to pass the time.

"Oh, dear, it's going to be a long wait. Are they all behind?" Mrs. Fielding had plumped herself down in the seat next to mine. "I can see we're going to be here half the morning."

"I'm afraid so," I said. "I've been here for ages already. Dr. Macdonald seems to be really slow this morning. When's your appointment?"

"Oh, I'm not here for the doctor. No, I've got to see Nancy Williams — now, she's a nice girl, really takes an interest in what you tell her — she's looking after my blood pressure and things."

"She is good, isn't she? Everyone seems to like her and she's very efficient."

"What I like about her" — Mrs. Fielding leaned forward confidentially — "is the way that when she doesn't know something, she says so right out and goes and asks one of the doctors. You wouldn't get most of the doctors doing that, now, would you?"

I smiled and nodded, not pointing out the flaws of logic in that statement.

"These nurse-practitioners, I think they're a really good idea. More human somehow —" She broke off and turned to look at someone who'd just come in. "Now, look at that, will you? A real disgrace."

I followed her gaze and saw a young man of about twenty. He had several days' growth of stubble, his nose and eyebrows were pierced, and his dark, greasy hair was caught back in a rubber band. He was wearing torn jeans and a black T-shirt with some sort of logo on it, which revealed arms that were heavily tattooed. He went over to reception and leaned on the counter.

Mrs. Fielding leaned closer again. "You know who that is, don't you?"

"I've seen him about the town," I said, "but I don't know his name."

"He's Rhys Hampden."

"Not — not Stephen and Monica Hampden's boy!"

"That's right. You wouldn't credit it, would you, such respectable people!"

"I don't know them very well, but yes, I am surprised he's their son."

"He used to be such a nice boy — they live quite near to me and I used to see him around, up and down the road. It all happened" — she lowered her voice — "when he went away to university. Not Oxford or Cambridge — one of those up in the Midlands somewhere — got in with the wrong set of people there. Drink and drugs and goodness knows what." She shook her head. "When I think of his poor parents and what a disappointment he must be to them!"

"How dreadful. But perhaps he's getting treatment. I mean, he's here to see one of the doctors, I suppose."

"Oh, they just come to get their drugs — well, not *proper* drugs, but something like

69

that. I think it's a disgrace, taking up the doctors' time like that, and all the expense."

"Still, if it helps them, surely that must be worthwhile."

Mrs. Fielding sniffed. "*If* it helps them."

Rhys Hampden had moved away from reception and sat down on one of the chairs near the door leading to the consulting rooms. I noticed with some amusement that the elderly lady who had been sitting in the chair next to him got up under the pretense of changing her magazine and then took another seat at the far end of the waiting room. Mrs. Fielding had noticed it too.

"I don't think it's nice having people like that in here, especially with elderly people. You never know what they might do." She motioned with her head to a notice on the wall about violence to medical staff. "And the doctors and nurses have enough to put up with, without any more troublemakers."

I was about to make some sort of mollifying remark when Nancy put her head round the door and called Mrs. Fielding in. I looked round the waiting room and calculated that there were about three people before me to see Dr. Macdonald, which at ten minutes a go (if I was lucky) meant another half an hour's wait. I wished passionately that I'd remembered to bring a book with me and got up to look through the scattered pile of magazines at the other end of the room. I managed to find an old copy of *Good Housekeeping* with some of the recipes torn out and tried to settle down again. After a short while Dr. Morrison came out and called in Rhys Hampden. I noticed that there was a perceptible lightening of the atmosphere when the young man had gone. He was in there for only a short time and when he came back through the waiting room he seemed agitated. I saw Lorna Spear leaning forward in the reception area to look at him as he passed through.

One more patient went in to Dr. Macdonald and I read an article about how some woman had restored a ruined house on Poros. As I looked at the pictures I wondered what her Greek neighbors thought of it all — the distressed (in every sense of the word) furniture, the violently colored hessian curtains and throws, the "amusing" objects scattered around and, especially, the examples of modern art that adorned the walls — but, then, I expect they're used to it all by now and think that everyone in England lives like that.

"Goodness, there's a lot of people waiting!" Susan Campbell came and sat beside me.

"I know," I said. "It's very slow this morning. When's your appointment?"

"I'm supposed to be seeing Dr. Morrison at half past," she said, putting her shopping bag down beside her. "I thought I was cutting it a bit fine, but I don't suppose he'll be through for a while yet."

"No, he's not too bad," I said. "I think there's only one more person before you. No, it's Dr. Macdonald who seems to be running late."

"Oh, good."

"How's Alan?" I asked. "Is he looking forward to his party?"

"He says it's all a lot of fuss — well, you know what men are like — but I think he's pleased really."

"Oh, I'm sure he is, and it's a nice way for his friends to say how glad they are that he's better."

She smiled. "Fiona's made him a birthday cake," she said. "She's a very good cook and she loves making something special like that."

"She's a very talented girl. I think it's wonderful the way she's settled down over here and I gather she's doing really well at her job."

"Oh, she loves it there," Susan said, "and they're a jolly crowd, so she's made some really nice friends."

The elderly man I'd identified as Dr. Morrison's next patient started to get restless. He got up and went over to reception and I heard him complaining (". . . been waiting here I don't know how long . . . not good enough . . . the NHS is going from bad to worse. . . .") and Lorna, although she was obviously speaking to him pretty sharply, looked worried, and when he reluctantly went back and sat down, I saw her pick up what I took to be the internal phone. After a minute she spoke to Valerie and Judith and went out through the door that led from reception to the consulting rooms.

"Oh, dear," I said, "I do hope there's not been another holdup — no one sent out on an emergency or anything. I really *don't* think I can bear waiting much longer."

"Do you think there's something wrong?" Susan asked.

"I don't know, but Lorna looked worried about something."

"Oh, dear, that is a nuisance. I've got a lot of shopping to do and I need to get Alan's lunch early because he's supposed to be going out for the afternoon with Mark Jackson. He said he'd come at about two thirty and take Alan for a drive. Alan's been so looking forward to it and I don't want to make him late."

"Oh, that's nice. Where are they going?"

"There's this fishing-tackle shop at Dulverton — Mark's mad about fishing and Alan thought he might take it up again. Mark's got a fishing license for Wimbleball Reservoir and he thinks Alan might like to go with him a couple of times to see if he likes it."

"What a good idea. Just what he needs, something out of doors but nice and peaceful. My father used to say that fishing was the best way of relaxing that he knew."

"He'll be glad to get out in the fresh air now the weather's warmer," Susan said. "He seems to have been shut up in the house for such a long time while he's been ill."

Out of the corner of my eye I saw Lorna going back into reception closely followed by Dr. Macdonald, both looking very upset. Alec Macdonald picked up the phone and I saw him speaking earnestly into it. When he put it down he came through into the waiting room. We all looked at him expectantly and for a moment he seemed disconcerted and unsure of what to say. Finally he began hesitantly.

"I'm afraid there's been an — an accident, and I'm sorry, but we're going to have to ask you to leave because we're having to close the surgery for the time being. I do apologize for the inconvenience — I know some of you have been waiting for a long time already. Lorna will come out in a minute and take your names and we will be in touch to give you alternative appointments. Thank you so much."

He went back into reception, leaving a buzz of conversation behind him.

"Well," Susan said, "what do you think all that was about?"

"He said an accident — but why have they had to close everything down? Very odd."

Lorna now appeared with a pen and clipboard. She was immediately besieged by questioning patients demanding to know what was happening, indeed, what *had* happened. The man who had been complaining before was particularly vociferous.

"It's a downright disgrace. I've been waiting days for this appointment and now they're just fobbing us off. Heaven knows when we'll finally get to see anyone. My chest's getting worse by the day. It'll be pneumonia before they'll do anything about it. People could die waiting to see someone. I'm certainly going to take this up with my M.P. . . ."

There were murmurs of assent from other

patients, and Lorna had a decidedly resentful reaction when she went round taking people's names.

"So what's happened?" I asked when she came to us.

"An accident, like Dr. Macdonald said," she replied. "I'm not at liberty to say anything more."

She took our names and passed on to the next patients.

Susan picked up her shopping bag. "Oh, well," she said, "I suppose I'd better get on to the supermarket."

"Did you want to see Dr. Morrison about anything important?"

"No, nothing that can't wait. How about you?"

"I just needed Dr. Macdonald to have a look at my wrist, but that can wait as well."

"I'd better get on," Susan said. "Are you coming?"

"I just want to pop into the chemist while I'm here, so I'll go out that way." I pointed to the door with the sign TO THE PHARMACY and made my way across the small graveled courtyard to the chemist next door. There I found several people who had been in the surgery engaged in animated conversation about the recent happening.

"You were there, weren't you?" One of the

women whom I knew by sight buttonholed me. "What did you make of all that?"

"I don't know," I replied. "They said there'd been an accident."

"That's what they *said,* but if it was just an accident, why did they have to close the place? Mr. Prothero here" — she indicated the elderly man who had been making a fuss — "he thinks it's something to do with drugs. You saw that dreadful young man who was in there. . . ."

"It might have been a robbery," Mr. Prothero broke in. "He might have attacked someone to get drugs — that's what they do. I wouldn't be surprised if it wasn't a case for the police."

"Surely not," I said. "Not in Taviscombe!"

But when I'd made my purchases and went outside I saw, as if on cue, a police car drawing up in the surgery car park and a police sergeant getting out.

"There you are, what did I say!" Mr. Prothero had materialized beside me. "A case for the police, that's what I said. It'll be drugs, you mark my words. That's what it is nowadays. Young people today don't know they're born. I went all through the last war, merchant navy, torpedoed twice. Soft, that's what they are, everything done for them.

And all this loud music, keeping decent people awake half the night!"

"It could just be an accident," I said. "The police might have to be called if it's serious."

"Well, drugs are serious," Mr. Prothero said. "There's nothing more serious than drugs."

We watched as the police sergeant walked towards the main surgery door and disappeared inside. For a moment we stood watching the door as if hoping for some further manifestation. Then Mr. Prothero said, "That's all they ever do nowadays, ride around in cars. When did you last see one on the street? In the old days there was a police house in every village and always a couple walking up and down the avenue. Now all you get are these traffic wardens and what use are they?" He looked at me sharply and when I didn't reply (and what could I have said?) he said, "Well, I can't hang about here all day. It's not good for my chest, all this standing about."

"No," I said. "I must get on."

He walked slowly away, pausing after a few steps to turn around and say, "It'll be drugs, just you mark my words."

After sitting for so long in the stuffy surgery I felt like a little sea air, so I drove down to the seawall beyond the harbor and stood for a while watching the waves creaming over the pebbles on the shore. I saw there was a new notice telling people not to feed the seagulls. THEY MAKE A MESS AND CAN BE VICIOUS. It was just the sort of officious notice I particularly dislike, so I was pleased to see that a large, raffish-looking seagull was perched on the top of the notice board, and I made a vow to bring them some stale bread next time I came down here.

I looked at my watch and saw that it was almost lunchtime, so rather than go home I decided to get something to eat at the Buttery. It was quite full, but easing my way through the crowd, I was glad to find a table for two in a corner and thankfully put down my tray. I was halfway through my quiche and salad (they do a very good Stilton and broccoli quiche) when I saw Valerie Carter at the counter. As she moved away I beckoned to her and she came over and sat down.

"Thank goodness," she said, "isn't it crowded! I suppose it's mostly holiday-makers. Everywhere is so full now that the season's started."

"I know. The supermarkets are quite impossible on some days, people with trolley-loads of beer and Coca-Cola — and as for Woolworths . . . !"

Valerie took a sip of her coffee. "It was my turn for an early lunch today," she said, "but I wasn't sure if I could go out. It's all been so confusing."

"What exactly has happened?" I asked tentatively.

"I don't know if I'm supposed to say anything. Still, it'll all be in the *Free Press* on Thursday, so I don't suppose it matters."

"Dr. Macdonald said it was an accident," I said. "Was it something serious?"

Valerie cut her sandwich carefully in half before replying slowly, "It is serious, yes, but no, they don't think it was an accident." She laid down her knife and looked at me. "It's Dr. Morrison. He's dead. They think he was murdered."

Chapter Six

"Murdered," I said, "but how?"

"He was stabbed," Valerie said with a shudder. "When it was a long time and he didn't come out for his next patient, Lorna went in to see if anything was wrong and she found him."

"How awful."

"She says she didn't realize at first what had happened — he was just sitting in his chair with his back to the door. But when she spoke to him and he didn't answer she went over and saw that he'd been stabbed. There was blood. . . ." Her voice trailed away.

"It must have been a terrible shock to her. To all of you," I said, looking at Valerie's pale face.

"Yes, it was rather." She pushed her sandwich away. "It doesn't seem real. I can't seem to take it in somehow."

"Look, drink some more of your coffee," I said. "Put lots of sugar in it — that's good for shock."

She obeyed me mechanically. "I feel rather awful about it," she said, "because I never really liked Dr. Morrison. He could be very sarcastic at times, and impatient when you didn't understand straightaway what he wanted. He made you feel a fool."

"He wasn't popular — I think a lot of people felt like you did."

"But now he's dead. . . ."

"You feel guilty that you disliked him. It's a very natural feeling, but it's not logical. Being dead — even being murdered — doesn't make someone a nicer person!"

She gave me a wintry smile. "You're right, of course, and as you say, quite a few people found him difficult to get on with. In the practice — I mustn't say, but, well, I expect you can imagine."

"Yes, I can. So what's happening — are the police still there?"

"They sealed off his room and all that corridor. I suppose they've got to do the whatever it's called — the forensics. They took statements from Judy and me — I think they're still doing the doctors. Like I said, it was my turn for an early lunch, but Dr. Macdonald said Judy and I should go home — the surgery's got to be closed anyway. I think they may want to ask Lorna about files and records and things, though, so she was going to stay." She finished her coffee. "I think I'd better get back home now. Mum was out, but I left a message on the answer phone telling her what's happened, so if she's back, she'll be worrying."

"Yes, of course. Can I give you a lift?"

"It's very kind of you, but it's not far, and really, I'd be glad of the fresh air."

The next day I had a visit from the police. Actually it was Constable Harris, whom I'd known ever since he was a small boy when he used to come with his father, who did our garden.

"Well, Bob," I said as he followed me into the sitting room, "I suppose it's about what happened at the surgery yesterday. Do sit down."

He sat down on the sofa, laying his peaked hat carefully on one of the arms.

"That's right, Mrs. Malory. We have to speak to everyone who was on the list they gave us of people who'd been in the waiting room. To see," he said, getting out his note-book, "if you *noticed* anything, if you get what I mean."

"Oh, dear, I'm sorry, I don't think I can be a lot of help, though I was there for rather a long time. Let me see. I last saw Dr. Morrison when he came into the waiting room to get that young man — what's his name? — Rhys Hampden."

"Did you see this Rhys Hampden come out?"

"Yes, after about ten minutes or so — maybe a bit less."

"And how did he seem?"

"Seem?"

"Did he look upset or anything?"

"Well, yes, he did a bit. Sort of agitated, and he went out of the surgery very quickly. Do you think . . . ?"

"It's early days yet," he said ponderously, "to be thinking anything. But we do need to check up on these things, you understand."

"Yes, of course."

"And was there anything else that struck you as odd? Anything about Dr. Morrison, for instance?"

"No — no, I don't think so. He seemed to be much as usual."

"Is he your doctor?"

"Oh, no, though I did see him once when Dr. Macdonald (he's my doctor) was away."

"And how did he strike you?"

"I'm sure he's very clever and probably a brilliant doctor in many ways, but he's not the easiest person."

"How do you mean?"

"Remote — I think that's the word that sums him up. I don't think he's very good with people, and that isn't a particularly good trait in a doctor."

"Not popular, then, would you say?"

"I wouldn't think so, but of course I don't really know much about him."

"So you wouldn't know if he had any enemies?"

"I'm sorry, I haven't the faintest idea. So this Rhys Hampden," I asked, "was he the last person to see Dr. Morrison?"

"As far as we know. What I mean is, he was the last person with an appointment. The trouble is" — he leaned forward and spoke confidentially — "that place is like a rabbit warren, so many doors in and out. For example," he continued, "you can get to the corridor where the doctors' surgeries are from three different ways as *well* as from the waiting room."

"Oh, dear, that must make things difficult for you."

"It's a nightmare, Mrs. Malory, a real nightmare."

"So anyone could have got in from outside and no one in reception or in the waiting room would have seen them?"

"That's right. It's all being built on a connecting square that does it, if you see what I mean. The corridor from the nurses' rooms goes round the quadrangle and meets up with the doctors' corridor. Then there's *another* corridor from that alternative-medicine place that joins the nurses' corridor. Then again, there's the back door — sort of staff entrance — that leads into reception and you can get from there straight into the doctors' corridor."

He paused for breath and I said sympathetically, "It really is impossible!"

He nodded. "Of course to get to the nurses' rooms you have to go through that back end of the waiting room, so I suppose people there would have seen who was coming and going."

"Not really, yesterday," I said, "at least not when I was there. Most people were at the other end — the doctors' end — even the people waiting to see the nurse, and they either had their heads buried in magazines or were talking to each other and wouldn't have noticed anything."

"Well," he said, picking up his cap, "I'd better go and see if they did."

"Sorry I wasn't any help," I said. "Can I offer you a cup of tea or coffee?"

"No, thanks, Mrs. Malory, I'd better get on."

"Well, do give my regards to your father. Tell him that winter-flowering cherry he planted was a picture last year."

Not surprisingly Dr. Morrison's death was one of the main topics of conversation at Alan's birthday party.

"It's very shocking, of course," Anthea said, "but he was a thoroughly disagreeable man."

"He was very reserved," Alan said, "and it took a long time to get to know him, but I always found him most sensible, and a very good doctor."

"Tell that to Moira Webster!" Anthea retorted. "Poor Kenneth should never have died like that."

"Oh, come, now," Alan said. "You can never really tell in cases like that."

"That's not what Moira thinks, and," she continued, "her son is still set on suing the practice. He's been to see a solicitor, I believe."

"Well, I speak as I find," Alan said. "Dr. Morrison certainly did all right by me. I wouldn't be here today if he hadn't sorted out that bypass. Don't you agree, Susan?"

"Oh, yes, he was wonderful — most efficient, he arranged everything so well and he was very good afterwards, taking care of Alan and following up on things."

"He always looks so miserable," Rosemary said. "*Dour* is the word for it, I think."

"Was he Scottish?" I asked. "I think Morrison's a Scottish name. Do we know where he came from?"

"Oh, London, I think," Susan said. "At least that's where he did his training."

"That's right," I said, "and he was part of a research team at one of the big teaching hospitals — Jean told me," I said to Anthea.

"She'll have come across him quite a lot in her job," Anthea said, "and, of course, being in the building at the time — the alternative-medicine part, that is — the police will have interviewed her."

"Oh, they're bound to have done," I said. "They came to see me. It was Bob Harris — you remember him," I said to Rosemary, "Eric Harris's boy. He's in the police now."

"That's right," she said. "Jack saw him when our car was damaged in that accident last year. A nice boy, he said."

"Why did the police want to see *you?*" Anthea asked.

"I was in the surgery, waiting to see Dr. Macdonald, when it happened."

"What were you seeing Dr. Macdonald about?" Anthea always likes to be informed of any unusual activity among her friends.

"Oh, only a check on my wrist. Jean said I should see him."

Anthea nodded. "Very sensible," she said.

"But I never did get to see him," I said, "because of Dr. Morrison getting killed. So now I'll have to try and make another appointment." I turned to Susan. "I suppose you will have to do the same. Only, of course, you'll have to see one of the other doctors now."

"Oh, I may not bother," she said. "It was only a checkup after my bronchitis and I'm quite all right now."

"Now, Susan," Alan said, "I do think you ought to see someone. You shouldn't take chances with your chest. She's never been the same since she went to Canada," he said to the rest of us, "all those bitter winters!"

"Well, I'll see," Susan said.

"It never does to ignore a bad chest," Anthea said. "It can lead to all sorts of things."

"If Dr. Morrison said you should have it checked, I think you should see somebody," Alan said. "He must have thought it was necessary or he wouldn't have said so. He was a man of few words, but when he said something he meant it."

"He was certainly very abrupt that day when we had the Hospital Friends meeting," Maureen Dawson said. She and her husband, Bruce, had been sitting in a corner eating vol-au-vents and sipping their drinks and had not, so far, taken much part in the conversation. "Almost rude, really, the way he rushed off like that and didn't stay for coffee. Well, you were there, Sheila. You saw how he was. But I believe he was like that. Janet — Janet Dobson, that is — was telling me that he was very unpopular in the practice. Her daughter, Lorna, works there and *she* says that most of them can't stand the sight of him."

"Thinks himself too good for general practice," Bruce broke in. "Always very *superior* the times I've had to see him, not really interested — he was very offhand about my carpal tunnel syndrome. Just prescribed ibuprofen and said it would go away. My brother, Jim, had an operation when *he* had it — they cut the nerve or something."

"And did it go away?" Rosemary asked.

"As it happened it did, but that's not the point. What I want to know is, why would he come down here to be a humble G.P. when he'd been some sort of hotshot on a research team in London?"

"I heard there'd been some sort of disagreement," I said, "though I'd have thought he could have found something else equally high-powered if he was that brilliant."

"Exactly!" Bruce said triumphantly. "It's all a bit fishy, if you ask me. And now he's gone and got himself murdered — what does *that* tell you?"

"*What* does it tell you?" Anthea asked impatiently. "I don't see someone coming down here from London especially to kill him. Apart from anything else, a stranger like that would have been spotted straightaway."

We all nodded in agreement, since Anthea always has any stranger spotted, summed up and filed away for reference within hours of his or her arrival.

"The police seem most interested in that young man Rhys Hampden," I said. "He was the last person to see Dr. Morrison — at least, he had the last appointment."

"There you are, then," Bruce said. "That's it."

"What do you mean?" Susan asked.

"He's a layabout and a druggie," Bruce said. "He'd have killed Morrison for not giving him any more drugs."

"I don't think doctors give them drugs, as such," Rosemary said.

"Well, whatever. No, you mark my words, that's what it'll be."

"It's his poor parents I'm sorry for,"

Maureen said. "Such nice people. And he had every advantage, went to university and everything."

"It's these universities that encourage them to behave like that," Bruce said. "Students nowadays! All doing these sociology courses and *media* studies, whatever that may mean!"

"Oh, I think there are some very nice young people doing sociology," Susan said. "Fiona's friend Katy is studying that at Bristol — I believe she's doing very well."

"Anyway," Bruce said, brushing this recommendation aside, "I don't think the police will have to look too far. That's if he hasn't run off."

"He certainly left in a hurry," I said.

"You saw him?" Maureen asked.

"Yes, like I said, I was waiting to see Dr. Macdonald. The young man looked upset and sort of rushed out. I remember thinking it was odd, but I'd been waiting so long I was in a bit of a daze — you know how you get — and didn't really take it in." I turned to Susan. "Did you see him, or was it before you arrived?"

"No, he must have gone by then."

"They'll have gone round to his house, then, the police," Bruce said, "to question him."

"It's his poor parents I feel sorry for," Maureen repeated. "Police cars outside the house and all the neighbors watching — it must be very upsetting for them."

"Pretty upsetting for Dr. Morrison," Anthea said sharply, "being killed like that." She turned to me. "Do we know how he was killed?"

"He was stabbed. Lorna found him."

"How awful for her!" Maureen said. "Fancy finding someone dead like that — it doesn't bear thinking about."

"He'll have picked up the first thing that came to hand," Bruce said, "that lad. Some sort of surgical instrument. When Morrison wouldn't give him any more drugs. It will have been a spur-of-the-moment thing, not premeditated."

"I don't know," Alan said, considering. "Are there surgical instruments lying about there, just like that?"

"Well, then," Bruce said, "he could have had a knife on him — they carry knives, don't they? I suppose we should be grateful it wasn't a gun and he'd had to shoot his way out."

"Actually," Rosemary said, "we don't know that it *was* Rhys Hampden who did it."

"Stands to reason," Bruce said. "Who else

would have had a motive for killing Morrison? It must have been him."

"Well," Alan said, "from what you've all been saying about the poor man, he had any number of enemies."

"Come, now, Alan," Anthea said, "all we've been saying is he wasn't well liked — most of us have had some sort of unpleasant experience with him. But just being unpopular, well, that's a far cry from murder."

"That's true," I said, "and there were probably lots of people, like Alan here, who thought he was a splendid doctor and were very grateful for what he did for them."

"Of course," Anthea said, "it could have been one of the other doctors — working together on top of each other at that surgery, there could easily be a motive there."

We were unable to investigate this theory further because Fiona came in just then with a large birthday cake, and as Alan blew out the single candle, we all gathered round and sang "Happy Birthday" in the stilted, embarrassed way that adults do.

Chapter Seven

When the surgery was open again, I was able to get another appointment. The waiting room was full, though whether with genuinely ill people or those who just wanted an excuse to view the scene of the crime, I don't know. It was a very hot day, unbelievably the ninth successive day of really hot weather we'd had. Unused to this Mediterranean climate, we were all becoming a trifle irritable and edgy and the children in the waiting room were whiny and fractious, while their mothers, some obviously at the end of their tether, were impatient and snappy. To get a breath of air in the surgery, all the doors were open, including the one onto the central courtyard, and I wondered if the staff felt very vulnerable after what had happened.

Valerie was back at work in reception.

"Hello, Mrs. Malory. I'm afraid we're running a bit late. Without Dr. Morrison . . ."

"Yes, of course. How are you?"

"Oh, I'm all right now, though we're all a bit shaken." She looked over her shoulder and leaned forward confidentially. "Lorna hasn't come in today. Actually, she hasn't been in since — since it happened."

"It's not surprising," I said, "after that sort of shock."

"She's been staying with her mother and *she* rang to say Lorna wouldn't be coming in for a bit."

"Quite understandable," I said, "though I suppose it makes you even more short-staffed, especially with so many patients to cope with."

"Yes, the phone hasn't stopped."

As if on cue the phone rang, Valerie turned away to deal with it, and I went and sat down near the open door to the court-yard. Looking across, I could see Joanna Stevenson walking along the far corridor. She was moving slowly, as if deep in thought, and as I watched, I saw her hus-band hurrying along the corridor obviously wanting to catch up with her. When he did they seemed to be arguing about something — he put his hand on her arm and she pulled violently away from him. Just at that moment one of the nurses opened the door of her office and Clive Stevenson turned abruptly and walked quickly away. I wondered what the quarrel had been about and if it had anything to do with John Morrison's death.

When I finally got to see Dr. Macdonald he was, not surprisingly, slightly distrait. He examined my wrist and seemed satisfied with the way it was healing.

"It wouldn't hurt to carry on with the physiotherapy for a bit," he said, "and I'm afraid it will never be quite what it was — there'll be less flexibility — but, on the whole, you've got off quite lightly."

"Just as long as I can use it," I said, "I won't fret about the flexibility. I was so sorry," I went on as I bent down to pick up my handbag, "to hear about Dr. Morrison."

"It's been very awkward," he said, "having to close the surgery like that. We were short-staffed before all this happened and now things are worse than ever. I really don't know how we're going to manage — it's very difficult to get a really reliable locum at this time of year."

Since Alec Macdonald was usually a kind, compassionate person, I was surprised that he expressed no actual regret at John Morrison's death, especially in such circumstances.

"Did he have any family?" I asked.

"There's an ex-wife and I believe there's

some sort of cousin. He never talked about himself — not to me at any rate. I don't even know who his solicitor was — the police wanted to know that."

"And he didn't have any friends? Among the other doctors, perhaps?"

Dr. Macdonald hesitated. "He didn't make friends easily. I believe he was only interested in his work." He got up as if to bring things to an end, and taking the hint, I left.

"He really didn't want to talk about it," I said to Thea that afternoon. "He seemed very uncomfortable when I mentioned it."

"Well, it was a murder after all, and he is the senior partner, so he must feel sort of responsible. Anyway, I imagine he felt he had to be discreet about one of his doctors — he couldn't go gossiping to his patients."

"I don't think I was *gossiping* exactly."

"No, but you know what I mean. A murder on the premises — he was just being careful what he said."

"Yes," I said doubtfully, "but it was more than that. Something to do with Morrison and the other doctors — I'm sure there've been problems there."

"I had gathered that he wasn't popular."

"Mmm, but I had the feeling that there was something specific, some special problem that Dr. Macdonald was brooding about. And then you see, not even a conventional expression of regret at his death, and such a violent death — *most* unusual from someone like him."

"He's probably just worried."

"I suppose."

Alice, who had been sitting at the kitchen table trying to fit some large jigsaw pieces together, in a moment of frustration lost patience with them, swept the whole lot onto the floor and burst into tears.

"Oh, dear," Thea said, gathering her up in her arms. "It's this heat — it doesn't suit her."

"Me neither," I said. "Tell you what, let's go down to the beach at Porlock Weir — there's always a breeze there. Would you like that, Alice — go paddling in the sea and have an ice cream?"

At the magic words the tears stopped. "Ice cream," Alice said, giving it a smile of approval. "Ice cream, Mummy, ice cream, Gran," she reiterated, as if to make sure that the concept was universally accepted.

There is no beach as such at Porlock Weir, that stretch of coast being composed mostly of shingle interspersed with large boulders, with a notable pebble ridge just beyond the harbor. However, at low tide a small stretch

99

of sand with miniature rock pools is uncovered, and since it is usually deserted, it is one of our favorite places. When I had seen Thea established on a comfortable boulder and Alice poking about in one of the pools with her spade, I went off to the small shop to get the ice creams.

The shop (which is also, in summer, a café noted for its excellent teas as well as sweets and newspapers) also sells basic groceries — tea, sugar, packets of cereals and so on — for the small population of the Weir who don't want the bother of driving into Porlock when they run out of these necessities. The shop was empty and Mrs. Lincoln, who kept it, was nowhere to be seen. I was leaning on the ice cream cabinet, trying to decide which of the many colorful varieties Thea and Alice would like, when a voice behind me said, "What an extraordinary coincidence — I've just been trying to ring you!"

It was my old friend Nora Burton. I've known Nora ever since we went up to Oxford from Taviscombe together. But while I returned home, she opted for London and a career as a high-flying civil servant. Her mother had died when Nora was quite young and her father never married again. He was the senior partner in a firm of solicitors in Taviscombe (my husband, Peter, did his Articles with him) and an enthusiastic yachtsman, which is why he had settled at the Weir in a house overlooking the sea and the harbor where his boat was moored.

Nora often visited him, and so we kept in touch over the years. She was devoted to her father and so I wasn't really surprised that when he had a stroke, she gave up her job and came back to look after him. Mr. Burton died several years ago and a lot of people thought that Nora would go back to her life in London, but she had stayed on in the old house, apparently contented, and now, I suppose, it's too late for her to make a move.

"It's been such ages since we had a really good chat," Nora said. "I rang to ask if you'd fancy coming to lunch."

"How lovely," I said. "When?"

"Tomorrow, if it's not too short notice. About twelve thirty?"

"I'd love to."

Mrs. Lincoln suddenly appeared from out of the back, saying, "Sorry m'dears — a couple of ramblers wanting cream teas. Now, what can I get you?"

"I got us all cornets," I said to Thea, handing her two of the already melting ice creams, "which was probably a mistake. Never mind, we can always wash off the stickiness in the sea!"

Next day the sun was still blazing down. The animals, who, in the winter, always crouch pathetically close to whatever source of heat they can find, now shunned the sun and both lay stretched out (Tris panting from time to time and Foss expressing total exhaustion by the occasional wearily lifted eyelid) on the relatively cool tiled floor of the kitchen, rousing themselves only to lap noisily from the various bowls of water I left around the house for them, and all the time regarded me reproachfully as the obvious author of their misery.

When you're over a certain age sleeveless garments can be a mistake, but it was so hot that I decided that comfort was more important than elegance and put on a dress with a camisole top that I had bought many years ago and had put away as being too youthful.

"I do deplore an expanse of middle-aged flesh," I said to Nora, "but in this weather!"

"I know. I can't imagine how those old women in Greece manage, swathed in black from head to foot."

"And think of those splendid Victorian

missionaries in Africa," I said, "all done up in whalebone and layers of petticoats!"

"I think it's because we're not used to *continuous* hot weather," Nora said, "day after day. We never really get used to it. Like being unprepared for winter — the way the first snow always comes as a surprise, as if we've never seen it before."

"I know. Still, I don't think I'd like to live in a predictable climate, would you? Think of not being able to talk about the weather every day!"

"I'd hate to miss the changing view I get from here," she said. We were standing by the window with our drinks, looking out on the seashore. "Those clouds, for instance, out over the sea, changing all the time, even on a day like this — I'd hate a permanently blue sky."

"You do love it here, don't you?" I said. "I used to wonder why you never went back to London and your exciting life there."

"Oh, I missed it dreadfully at first, and almost resented being here — not being with Father of course, but being out of the world like this."

"But?"

"After Father died I went up to London occasionally, but I was always glad to come back home. I knew I'd never leave."

"Do you still miss your London life, your work and your friends?"

"I did in the beginning. I was restless and bored and some of my friends dropped away and we lost touch. But I made new friends and" — with a smile at me — "rediscovered old ones, and looking round, I found plenty to occupy me — peaceful things like gardening or walking Barney here." She patted the placid golden Labrador that lay at her feet.

"That's nice," I said.

"Actually I didn't lose all my London friends. John Morrison bought a house here — almost next door."

"You knew John Morrison? I'm so sorry. I had no idea — it must have been awful for you."

"His death was a terrible shock. John was a very dear friend. In fact, it was because of me that he moved down here in the first place."

"Good heavens. Had you known him long?"

"About ten years, I suppose. I met him at a dinner party given by Daphne Tyler — I think you met her once when you came up to London. She was quite a bit younger than me and had only just joined the ministry from COI. A small, dark girl with enormous brown eyes."

"Oh, yes, I remember her."

"She had quite a thing about John. He'd just broken up with his wife and I suppose she thought she might have a chance."

"And did she?"

"No, John was absolutely shattered when Virginia left him — it was a very messy business, all mixed up with their work. The last thing he wanted then was another relationship. No, we sort of hit it off that evening — we had a lot in common — and we began to see each other for meals and theaters. Just as friends. I was that much older and he — well, I think he wanted, not exactly a shoulder to cry on (he wasn't that sort of person), but just someone to be *with,* if you see what I mean. A sort of friend, in fact."

"I see."

"He came down with me when I visited Father and *they* hit it off too. They both loved sailing and John used to come down on his own sometimes to crew for Father. So when there was this trouble with the research group and he felt he had to leave, he decided to come down here and join the practice in Taviscombe. A house on the Weir was vacant, so he bought it and moved in."

"What sort of person was he?" I asked. "Somehow I find it difficult to think of him as anyone's friend — I suppose because he seemed so *remote*."

Nora smiled rather sadly. "He was always what you might call reserved — something to do with being a Lowland Scot perhaps — but there was warmth there and wit and humor. And, of course, a formidable intellect. Sometimes I got angry with him for burying himself away down here when he should have been out in the world doing something really important."

"What happened? I mean, with the London research team?"

"It was complicated — there was this man, Paul Sutton, very brilliant in his field, but very, very ambitious. You know, a Nobel Prize always in his sights. Because he had an easy manner, easier than John certainly, he got everyone on his side, especially the professor who was leading the team, who thought Sutton was something really special — you know how some people can create an *impression*."

I nodded. "I know what you mean."

"Well, John had made quite a bit of progress in one aspect of the research, and like a fool, he discussed it with Sutton, used him as a sort of sounding board, but being John, cautious and truly scholarly, he wouldn't share it with anyone else until he'd got the whole thing completed. You can guess what happened. Sutton, using John's work, forged ahead along those lines and, not being as thorough as John, got the results written up first and presented them as his own."

"Good heavens."

"John was appalled — not just by the false claim, but because, although the general principle was right, the working out, as it were, was careless and badly done, so much so that he felt it vitiated the strength of the theory."

"How awful. But couldn't he prove that this Sutton had stolen his work?"

"Not really, there was no sort of time-scale. Sutton implied that he'd been working along those lines for ages before John and that John had been more or less following in his footsteps. He was popular, you see, so everyone wanted to believe him. John, being a forthright sort of person who didn't suffer fools gladly, was not."

"So unfair!"

"The worst thing was that Virginia, who was also working on the team, sided with Sutton."

"But she was his wife — hadn't John told her what lines he was working on?"

"No, like I said, he was a perfectionist. He

had to get things absolutely right before he'd present them. Besides, there was a sort of rivalry between them. He was the brightest, no doubt about that, but Virginia found it hard to accept. There was an edge there."

"That's terrible."

"The final blow came when he discovered that Virginia and Sutton had been having an affair."

"Which is why she sided with him."

"Exactly. I can't imagine how he must have felt — utterly disillusioned about the work and devastated by the breakdown of his marriage. But I understood why he wanted to get away, to leave all that sort of thing behind him."

"You were a good friend to him."

Nora shook her head. "Not really. If you think about it, if I hadn't persuaded him to come down here, then he might still be alive today."

Chapter Eight

I shook my head. "You mustn't think like that. It was fate, karma, bad luck, whatever — but it certainly wasn't your fault. You were the person who gave him another chance. I'm sure he was grateful for that."

Nora shrugged. "I can't help feeling guilty. Yes, in a way he was better when he was down here, not so bitter and miserable. I think he might have been able to make a sort of life for himself, if only . . ." Her voice trailed away.

"Have you seen the police? Do they have any idea who might have been responsible?"

"A Sergeant Harris came and asked me questions the day after it happened, just generalities. Then I had a visit from some sort of higher-up CID man, Eliot, I think the name was. I have his card somewhere."

"Oh, that's Roger. He's Rosemary's son-in-law, very nice and most efficient — I'm very fond of him. What did he say?"

"When he discovered that we were friends

as well as neighbors, he wanted to know about John as a person and all about his life in London, the things I've just told you."

"He didn't say how they were getting on?"

"No, just that inquiries were 'ongoing,' which could mean anything."

"Do you have any *idea* — I mean, do you think it was someone local, or someone from his life in London? And *why?* I gather he wasn't exactly popular with the other doctors here, but dislike is one thing. Murder, surely, is another!"

She shook her head. "I can't imagine anyone wanting to kill John. But then, I suppose that's because I was his friend and I saw a side of him that he didn't let other people see."

"He was a loner, then," I said tentatively, "only interested in his work — that's what Dr. Macdonald said."

Nora hesitated for a moment. "You know I said he might have been able to make a new life for himself. Well, there was someone he seemed fond of, a sort of relationship."

"Really, who?"

"I don't know her name. John just called her Jay. I gather she was married — I think she was going to divorce her husband to be with John. He wouldn't say any more and I respected his reserve. He would have told me when things were sorted."

"Did you ever see her?"

"I saw her car parked outside sometimes, but I never actually saw *her*. Besides, I would have hated John to think that I was spying on him."

"Do you think she had something to do with — with his murder? Her husband, perhaps?"

"It's possible."

"Did you tell Roger Eliot?"

Nora frowned. "I couldn't betray his confidence," she said.

"But if it helped to find his killer?"

"No, John wouldn't want her dragged into this."

"Fair enough."

"There is something else," she said hesitantly. "It may be nothing to do with it, but it was strange and somehow disturbing."

"Really?"

"Someone was — what do they call it now? — someone was stalking him."

"Good heavens!"

"A youngish woman — in her thirties, I'd say. She used to hang about outside the house watching for him to come home."

"Did he know her?"

"Oh, yes. She sent him letters and presents — it was all very difficult and unpleasant."

"Who was it?"

"Again, he never told me her name. He used to call her the Incubus — he tried to make a joke of it, but I could tell that he found it distressing."

"I suppose it might be one of the hazards of being a doctor, having female patients fixated on you."

"Women did find him attractive — you know, tall, dark, slightly forbidding."

"Yes, I can see that, though Mr. Rochester rather than Mr. Darcy, don't you think?"

Nora smiled. "He would have been horrified to hear you compare him to a romantic hero."

"Did you see her — the Incubus? I suppose you must have done if she was hanging about outside."

"Yes, I did. Very ordinary, longish brown hair, glasses, short, quite smartly dressed. Something about her looked familiar — I suppose I must have seen her around in the town. I'd certainly recognize her if I saw her again."

"I wonder if she is a patient," I said thoughtfully, "or even someone from the surgery. What a pity you go to the Porlock practice — you might have recognized her if she is. Did you tell the police about her?"

"No. I suppose I should have done, but it seemed like betraying his confidence. He was such a private person and there's something — I can't explain it, something undignified about being stalked."

"Surely," I said, "it's the stalker, not the stalked, who's undignified. But she might be unbalanced — they often are — and sometimes they kill or injure the person they're obsessed with."

"You're right, of course. I should have told the police. I'll ring this man Eliot." She turned away from the window. "Anyway, lunch is ready — let's go in. I want to hear all about Michael and Thea — and, of course, Alice."

The hot weather went on, day after scorching day, and I formed the habit of walking along the beach at Taviscombe whenever I went in there to do my shopping. Even when there wasn't much of a breeze, just looking at the water somehow made me feel cooler. In spite of it being the holiday season, the far end of the beach is never crowded, just a few locals either fishing at high tide or dog-walking when the tide is out.

I was wandering along aimlessly, watching the gulls swooping in circles, and one smaller one in particular — a tern, perhaps, I'm never sure — standing there opening and shutting its mouth as if in a silent cry.

"I've often wondered why they do that."

A voice behind me made me turn round and I saw it was Roger Eliot.

"Roger, hello! What are you doing here at this time of day?"

"Day off, so I thought I'd go for a walk — too hot to stay indoors."

"Isn't it awful? Though I suppose when the winter comes we'll look back in longing."

"I was just thinking of paddling in the sea. I bet the water's still cold. It would take more than this little heat wave to warm up the Bristol Channel. But it doesn't look particularly appealing."

We both turned and looked at the small waves curling onto the beach. The water was the usual reddish brown (the result of the red earth washed down into the channel from the rivers that run into it) with a scummy froth that lay unappetizingly on the hard sand.

I laughed and shook my head. "No, I don't think so. It's funny, though — when I was a child we always bathed here and never seemed to notice how uninviting the water looked."

"Oh, well, children never do. Though Delia and Alex seem to prefer swimming pools. But it's not the same. There's something about actually being *in* the sea — oh, well, we'll have to wait for abroad. Are you going anywhere this year?" he asked.

"No, I can't be bothered to arrange anything and then there's the problem of putting the animals in kennels — not to mention the fact that it's even hotter abroad. No, if only we had our usual English summer weather, I'd be perfectly happy to stay where I am. How about you?"

"The school holidays coming when they do, it's never worth it — too hot and crowded. No, we all went to Italy at Easter — Lake Como. It was a great success — even the children liked it. I'll try and take some time off when they're on holiday and we'll do a few excursions. Just at the moment, though, we're a bit tied up with this Morrison case." He turned and looked at me quizzically. "I'm surprised you haven't mentioned it, since you were actually there when it happened. Yes, I've seen the reports and lists of people on the scene."

"Well, yes, as it happens, I was. And, yes, I was going to ask you about it."

He laughed. "Go ahead."

"What about Rhys Hampden? Have you questioned him?"

He shook his head. "Unfortunately, no. When Sergeant Harris went to call on him he wasn't there. He's run off somewhere and we haven't found him yet."

"Does that mean . . . ?"

"That he killed Dr. Morrison? It's not quite that simple. Yes, Rhys was the last patient to see him, and yes, he did leave the surgery in a hurry."

"He certainly did. I saw him go."

"And I suppose that should make him the prime suspect."

"But?"

"There's something about it that doesn't feel right."

"But surely, Dr. Morrison wouldn't give him the methadone, or whatever the stuff is, and he got worked up and stabbed him."

"How do you know Dr. Morrison was stabbed?"

"Valerie told me. I just happened to see her after. She was very upset and told me."

"Just happened? Come, now, Sheila, I know you better than that! Anyway, the thing is, it was totally out of character."

"But surely people on drugs do behave out of character."

"True, but he was a very gentle, timid sort of boy. His parents said he seemed to be really frightened about something — they didn't seem surprised that he had run anyway — nothing to do with the murder, just running away from something, or someone."

"Still . . ."

"But there was another thing too. There was only one wound, and that was in a vital spot. Of course it might have been a lucky shot, as it were, but it could also mean that the murderer had some medical knowledge and knew exactly where to strike."

"And where better," I said, "to find someone with medical knowledge than in a doctors' practice?"

Roger shrugged. "It is possible."

"Well," I said, "that opens up the field a bit."

"There was something else," Roger continued. "The wound was a strange shape. It'd been made with an unusual blade — curved. Now, that isn't exactly the kind of weapon a boy like Rhys would be carrying."

"Could it have been some sort of surgical instrument that he — or someone else — snatched up from the desk?"

"I asked the various doctors if there was

such an instrument, something that would leave that sort of wound."

"And?"

"I got a variety of answers. There were several instruments that it could be. But the conclusion was that whatever it might have been, it was something unusual and certainly not the sort of thing that would be lying about in a G.P.'s surgery."

"So the murderer would have brought it with him."

"And since we didn't find anything there that fitted its description, he (or she) took it away afterwards."

"So no help."

"No, I'm afraid not." There was a pause while we both looked out to sea, considering the implications of that. Then Roger said, "Sheila, how well did you know this man Morrison?"

"Hardly at all. I met him a few times and formed a sort of opinion of him, but I'm beginning to think I may have got him wrong."

"In what way?"

"He's the sort of man I instinctively dislike — brusque, impatient, arrogant, very sure of himself — a stereotype really."

"But you changed your mind?"

"Sort of. I think he was more complicated than that. Also, I find that an old friend of

118

mine, whose judgment I trust, was very fond of him, so there must have been a side to him that wasn't immediately apparent."

"I'm getting very mixed messages about him from the doctors at the surgery."

"Why? What do they say?"

"A couple of the men felt as you did — found him difficult to get on with. I got the impression he didn't suffer fools gladly."

"That's what my friend Nora said."

"Nora? Nora Burton, out at Porlock Weir?"

"That's right. I gather you've spoken to her."

"Mm, yes. She was perfectly civil and all that, but I had the feeling she wasn't telling me everything she knew. Am I right?"

I hesitated. "She said she felt a sort of loyalty to his memory, not to talk about his private life, but there is something I think is important and I believe I persuaded her to get back to you."

Roger shook his head. "Thank you, Sheila. I suppose you don't feel like telling me yourself? No, I thought not, but if she *doesn't* come back to me, I'll be back to you!"

"You said there were mixed feelings about him among the other doctors. Who stuck up for him?"

"Dr. Macdonald, of course. I suppose he would, really, being the head of the practice. But I felt he genuinely liked Morrison and was full of admiration for his capabilities. He said they were very fortunate to have someone of his caliber in the practice and that he should, by rights, have been doing high-powered research. Which, I gather, is what he had been doing before he came down here."

"Nora told me about that. I expect you've heard all about the problems with the research team and why he left."

"Yes. It sounds like a messy business, but that was in London — I don't think it's really going to be relevant to us."

"You think it was someone local?"

"It seems most likely. After all, it had to be someone who knew the layout of the building." He sighed. "It could hardly be more difficult. You'd think, wouldn't you, that their security would have been better?"

"Security is all very well, but if it was someone who had a right to be there — a patient or one of the staff, or a doctor — then it wouldn't have been all that much of a help. Unless it's something really unusual — like Rhys Hampden rushing out like that — you don't really take much notice of what's going on around you. Especially in a doctor's waiting room, where everyone's absorbed in their own affairs and problems."

"True. Did you see Dr. Morrison that day?"

"Only when he came out to fetch a patient."

"Did he look different in any way?"

"No, I don't think so, but, like I said, I wasn't paying attention to anything very much."

"He had quite a full list of people to see, apparently. Presumably because he was only in a couple of days a week."

"I know. Alan — my friend Alan Johnson, who's a patient of his — is always complaining about how difficult it is to get an appointment with him. Mind you, Alan thinks — thought — he was absolutely brilliant, and wouldn't dream of seeing anyone else. I gather Dr. Morrison was doing some sort of research project that the practice was sponsoring."

"Yes, something to do with genetics. It was a nationwide thing, but I haven't got the details yet — that's something I have to go into. I suppose there just might be a connection with the London research, though that's a bit of a long shot."

"You said that some of the men disliked him. What about the women?"

"They all said how brilliant he was, but they didn't seem to have had much to do with him as a person. Still I suppose that's not surprising, since he didn't seem to mix socially with any of them. The nurses and the nurse-practitioner didn't say much at all. I got the impression that they were a bit scared of him."

"I'm not really surprised. I should think he was quite formidable to work with."

"Oh, well," Roger said, "I suppose I'd better be getting back. I promised Jilly I'd be in for lunch." He turned and looked at the sea. "Pity it's not crystal clear and Mediterranean blue."

"Come, now," I said, laughing, "as a true Charlotte M. Yonge enthusiast you must remember what she said about it. Don't you remember in *Hopes and Fears* when she brings Owen and Lucilla down here for a holiday after their father had died? She wouldn't 'brook hearing much about the hue of the Bristol Channel' and I gather it looked just as muddy in her day!"

"Oh, well, it's nice to know that some things don't change," Roger said, turning to go back up the steps to the promenade. "Remember — I do need to know anything at all that might help with this murder."

I walked a little farther along the beach.

Then, on an impulse, I took off my sandals and walked across the ribbed sand several feet into the sea.

Chapter Nine

When I opened the medicine cabinet, and a tube of antiseptic cream, some insect repellent and a packet of plasters fell out into the bath, and when I tried to put them back again and couldn't close the door, I knew it was time to have a proper clear-out. I loathe sorting out all cupboards, and medicine cupboards are particularly depressing. I took everything out — the sticky bottles of cough mixture, the half-used shampoos that *hadn't* given me the shiny, bouncy hair promised by the television advertisements, the ancient tablets of soap, the curiously shaped eye bath, the old toothbrushes I was going to use to clean awkward corners with — the whole useless clutter, in fact, that you keep because you can't be bothered to throw it away.

I'd just finished wiping down the shelves and rearranging the few items worthy of being kept when the phone rang. It was Nora.

"I've seen the Incubus," she said.

"Really? Where?"

"Martha Collins — you know, she lives next door — asked me if I'd take her mother into Taviscombe to see her doctor, only Martha's car's being repaired and you know how unreliable taxis are. So I said I'd take her in and wait to bring her back. Anyway, their doctor is Dr. Macdonald, so I took her into the surgery and there was the Incubus — she was the receptionist on duty!"

"Good heavens!"

"And while I was waiting I heard one of the other girls there call her Lorna."

"No!"

"Do you know her?"

"Yes, I do and I've known her mother for years — you may remember her, Janet Dobson."

"Sort of rings a bell. Wasn't she that rather unpleasant girl who stole Marjorie Fraser's boyfriend?"

"So she did, I'd forgotten. But typical, though. Lorna's just like her, disagreeable and bossy. We weren't at all surprised when her husband — Ronald Spear, rather a nice man but a bit dim — left her. Fancy her stalking Dr. Morrison. Goodness, I've just remembered. . . ."

"Remembered what?"

"She was the one who found him."

"Found him?"

"When he didn't come out for ages to collect his next patient she went in — just like her to want to know what was going on — to see what had happened."

"Poor girl."

"Yes. It must have been especially horrible for her, feeling as she did. She certainly looked upset, but I didn't take all that much notice because they just said there'd been an accident, and she seemed all right when she came round and took all our names."

"Names?"

"Of people in the waiting room who'd need new appointments. But apparently she didn't go into work for days afterwards. When I heard that, I thought she was just being a drama queen, but now — now I can see why. She must have been devastated. Unless . . ."

"Unless?"

"Unless she killed him. It's a possibility, you know. Nora," I said earnestly, "you really *must* tell Roger Eliot about her. You do see that?"

"I suppose so."

"And about this woman Jay as well. No," I went on as she started to protest, "it's too important not to. Roger's very discreet.

Nothing will come out about anyone's private life that isn't absolutely relevant to the investigation."

"Of course." Nora's voice was suddenly decisive. "You're right, and I believe it's what John would have wanted me to do. He used to say that in science and in life the facts were what mattered."

I happened to see Valerie a few days later when I was in the library.

"How are you?" I asked. "It must still be very difficult for you all at the surgery."

"We're still extra busy, but Dr. Macdonald's managed to get hold of a locum. He's Dutch but very nice and he speaks really good English."

"I think most people in Holland do — I suppose they have to because nobody really learns Dutch, do they? What's his name?"

"Dr. van der Meer."

"He sounds more like a painter than a doctor, but I'm sure you'll be very glad to have him."

"Oh, yes, it's made quite a difference already."

"How is Lorna?"

She looked at me questioningly.

"I was thinking, it must have been terrible for her — finding the body like that. And I believe you said she was away from work for several days."

Valerie nodded. "She was really in a state. Not at first, but after all the patients had gone it suddenly seemed to hit her and she more or less collapsed."

"Really?"

"Dr. Macdonald said it was some sort of hysterical reaction. He gave her a sedative and took her home — well to her mother's — himself. That was after the police had gone."

"They didn't question her, then?"

"Oh, no. Dr. Macdonald said she wasn't in a fit state. I think they went to see her at home, though."

"Still, I don't suppose there was much that she could tell them, was there? I mean, when she found him like that, I expect she just turned and ran away. I know I would."

"Actually," Valerie said, "she didn't — run away, that is. She said she was so shocked she just stood there. She couldn't believe it. Then, when she touched him and found blood on her hand, she sort of came to. But she was still in a daze when she got back and told us. It was only later, like I said, that she really broke down, sobbing as if her heart would break. It was dreadful."

"She must be very highly strung," I said.

"Of course it would be a terrible shock to find someone murdered, but well . . ."

"I wasn't that surprised." Valerie leaned towards me and lowered her voice. "She had a bit of a crush on Dr. Morrison. In fact she was really keen."

"And did he . . . ?"

"Oh, no. Nothing like that. Never spoke to her except in the way of work — well, you know how sort of *remote* he was."

I reflected how often that word was used to describe him, as if it was all people could think of to say about him. "Yes, he was," I said. "Do you know if there *was* anyone?"

"Did he have a girlfriend?"

"Well — yes."

"Oh, I don't think so. Not that we'd have known — he'd never have let on. But I suppose that's why Lorna sort of hoped. You know, if there wasn't anyone else, she might have a chance." She laughed. "Not very likely. Lorna isn't good-looking and she's got a rotten temper." She looked at her watch. "I've got to go. I'm on the afternoon shift — the Mother and Baby Clinic — it gets a bit noisy in the waiting room sometimes! Nice to have seen you, Mrs. Malory."

I stood for a while, leaning against the biography section, thinking about what Valerie had told me. More than ever it seemed important that Nora should tell Roger about Lorna and, indeed, about everything she knew (or surmised) about his private life. I wondered what the police had found in his house when they searched it, as they must have done. I made a mental note to ask Nora what she knew about that. Poor Lorna, how terrible it must have been for her — but then, how even more terrible if she had actually killed him.

"Excuse me." Someone behind me reached up to take a life of the Queen Mother off the shelves and I moved away. Pausing only to look crossly at the banks of computers that seemed to be taking over more and more of the book space, I left the library and drove home.

Nora rang me again that evening.

"The police have released John's body," she said, "so I'm arranging his funeral."

"You are?"

"There's no one else really. I believe there's some sort of second cousin up in Scotland, but I wouldn't have the faintest idea of how to get in touch with him."

"Was there a solicitor?"

"It was a London firm. I suppose they might know if he mentioned this cousin in his will, but it would all take too long. And I don't imagine Virginia will want to do anything. No, I'll arrange things — it's the last thing I can do for John."

"Yes, I can see that."

"I was just ringing to ask if you'd come — I'd be really glad of your support."

"Of course I will. When is it?"

"Next Friday, St. Decumen's, two o'clock. The afternoon seemed best so that if any of the doctors want to come, it will be after morning surgery."

"Would he have wanted a church service, do you know?"

"I think so. We never really talked about such things, but he was a son of the manse — his father was a minister up in Scotland — and I think he still had certain feelings. So I felt I had to give him a Christian burial, as it were, just to be on the safe side."

" 'Some says the prayer don't do no good / But there, don't do no harm,' " I quoted from a famous West Country monologue.

Nora laughed. "My sentiments exactly," she said. "Anyway, thank you for saying you'll come. I've arranged for a sort of gathering afterwards at the hotel at the Weir — drinks and sandwiches, I suppose. It's an awkward time of day, but I felt I had to do something to round it off."

The church was quite full. Most of the

doctors were there: Dr. Macdonald, of course, with Dr. Porter and Dr. Howard from the other practice, together with Nancy, the nurse-practitioner, and two of the other nurses. Valerie and Ann, another receptionist, were there as well, but not Lorna. They all sat together at the front. Brian Norris was there too ("Representing the Hospital Friends," I heard him say to the undertaker's man who was taking names at the door). Quite a good turnout for someone respected but not liked. After a while Joanna Stevenson came in, but she was alone (I suppose Clive Stevenson was holding down the fort at the surgery) and she sat near the back, not with the others. Presently Alan and Susan came in and sat by me.

"We felt we had to come and pay our respects," Alan said. "Fiona would have come too, but she couldn't really get time off work."

We all stood up as the coffin came in. It was followed by Nora and another woman, whom I took to be Virginia, and, to my surprise, Mr. Wheeler. As I listened to the familiar words of the service — it was the proper Prayer Book service — I covertly studied Virginia. She was tall, as tall as John Morrison had been, fashionably dressed (in gray, a compromise, perhaps, between the black of a widow and the muted colors of a mere friend), with sleek, dark hair worn rather too long. Beside her, Mr. Wheeler, presumably in deference to the occasion, had smoothed down *his* hair and looked much older than when I had seen him last.

As we all rose to go out into the church-yard I saw that Joanna Stevenson had gone. I imagine she'd wisely seated herself in a position to make an unobtrusive exit if one of the minor emergencies of pregnancy over-took her. The rest of us took up our places round the grave. The heat wave had broken with a thunderstorm and now, several days later, the air was fresh with a slight breeze blowing. The rector's voice was loud in the open air: ". . . And we meekly beseech thee, O Father, to raise us from the death of sin unto the life of righteousness. . . ."

I wondered if the murderer was one of those gathered round the grave and how he (or she) would react to those words. But all the faces around me wore that identical ex-pression of solemnity people assume on such occasions. Earth was scattered on the coffin, and a wreath of white roses placed at the foot of the grave, and we all dispersed slowly as if reluctant to be seen the first to break away.

"Are you going to this do at the hotel?"

133

Alan asked. "Only if you are, then I wonder if you could give me a lift back. Susan's got to get back to Taviscombe and I'm still not driving. . . ."

"Of course," I said. "I'd be delighted." We walked slowly to where I'd left the car. "I do want to be there for Nora. I can't remember if you know her or not."

"Slightly — I knew her father, a marvelous old gentleman, but that was before she came back down here."

"Nora was a good friend to Dr. Morrison," I said, "after his marriage broke up. I think that must have been his ex-wife who was with her at the funeral. I must say I'm a bit surprised she came."

When we got to the hotel, though, Virginia had somehow assumed the role of hostess and chief mourner, shaking hands with people and thanking them for coming. I went over to Nora, who was standing in the background, ironically watching this performance.

"Typical of Virginia," she said, "always has to be center stage."

"I think it's awful," I said indignantly. "You made all the arrangements — anyhow, I don't know how she has the nerve to be here at all, after the way she treated him!"

Nora shrugged. "Nerve isn't something

134

she was ever short of. She never was one for admitting she was in the wrong. In fact it wouldn't surprise me at all if she expected John to have left her something in his will, even though she got half the money from the house."

"She sounds absolutely ghastly," I said.

"Not my favorite person."

I looked around at the various people helping themselves to refreshments.

"I was surprised to see Mr. Wheeler. Was he a friend or a colleague? And," I added, "he seems to be friendly with Virginia." I indicated the two of them deep in conversation in a corner.

"They all trained together," Nora said. "Virginia, John, and Francis Wheeler — they were all on Sir Geoffrey Bailey's team at Barts. The brightest of their year. That's how John and Virginia met — more's the pity. I think Francis had a bit of a thing about her then, but that was over long ago. He's married to someone half his age. I think he likes to think of himself as young and trendy — a bit sad, really."

"It was a good congregation," I said. "You must be very pleased."

"Yes, I wanted to do it properly. Even," she said with a wry smile, "if it means Virginia taking over."

In the car driving home, Alan said, "Sad, wasn't it, that there were no relatives? I don't count that ex-wife of his, a nasty piece of work, I should say. I always think it's one of the saddest things there is to have no one to call your own at the end."

"I know," I said, falling back behind a caravan that was swaying rather erratically over the road. "We're lucky."

"You've got young Michael and Thea and little Alice. They'd never let you down."

"No, bless them, I don't think they would."

"It was always a sadness to Mary and me that we never had children and when my poor Mary died, I couldn't believe my luck when Susan said she'd come home to be with me. There'd been a falling-out in the family. You wouldn't remember it — you were too young. There was this fuss when she wanted to marry Jim Campbell and go off to Canada with him. Susan was barely twenty and he was much older. My father put his foot down and said she couldn't go — well, you weren't of age until you were twenty-one in those days. But she went all the same and he never forgave her — my mother was very upset, but she'd never go against Father. I was away in the Middle East then — I hadn't seen Susan since she was a little girl — so I missed it all."

"I never knew that. So what happened?"

"Well, a little while after my parents died I came home to England and some years after that, I had a letter from Susan saying that Jim had died and couldn't we keep in touch? She said how much she missed the family."

"That was nice."

"One of the best things that's ever happened to me," Alan said, "and Fiona too — well, it's as if she's my own. No, I've been very blessed and that's why it grieves me that a good man like John Morrison should have gone out of this world with no one of his own to grieve for him."

"Nora grieves for him," I said, "but I do see that however many friends you have, and however loving they are, it's not the same as family."

Was John Morrison a good man? I wondered as I made myself a cup of tea when I got home. He was brilliant — everyone agreed about that — but good? There must have been something good about him for Nora to be his friend. I wished that I'd known him, properly as a person, not just casually as a doctor, so that I could know what he was really like and understand why someone hated him enough to kill him.

Chapter Ten

I'd just finished changing the bed — something I try to do when Foss is out of the way, since he always wants to join in, and changing a duvet cover with a cat inside it is not easy — when there was a ring at the door. It was Roger.

"Sorry to arrive unannounced," he said, "but I was passing the end of your lane, so I thought I'd call to tell you the latest."

"Come in," I said. "Tea or coffee?"

"Coffee, please."

He followed me into the kitchen and sat down at the table while I put the coffee on.

"I also want to thank you," he said.

"Thank me?"

"I had a visit from your friend Nora Burton. I imagine that was your doing."

"Well," I said virtuously, "I did say I thought she should tell you everything she knows."

Roger regarded me quizzically. "*Everything* she knows?" he inquired.

"Of course." I got out the biscuit tin and

put some chocolate digestives on a plate. "So what's happened?" I asked.

"To begin with, we've got Rhys Hampden. The Bristol police found him. He was living in a squat and frightened to death, poor lad."

"Frightened?"

"Apparently he owed some local drug dealers money and they'd been threatening him. That's why he was so upset when Dr. Morrison refused to give him any more methadone — he's already had his proper amount. He'd planned to give it to the dealers in return for a little more time to pay them. When he couldn't do that he just ran away."

"And you don't think he had anything to do with the murder?"

"I'm pretty sure he didn't."

"Not even in a panic?"

"Not really. I don't think he had it in him, and, anyway, there's still the problem of the weapon. None of the doctors can think of any instrument that would make that sort of wound lying about in the surgery."

"So what's happening about Rhys?"

"His parents are getting him on a drug rehab scheme. We should come down on him pretty hard for bolting like that — wasting police time and so forth — but thanks to him, we've been able to clean up a local drug cell."

I poured the coffee and pushed the plate of biscuits towards him. "So that was a dead end — now what?"

"Well, thanks to your friend Nora, we do have a couple of new leads."

"A couple?"

"Well, I'll certainly be having a word with this Lorna Spear. If she really has been stalking Dr. Morrison, it could have led to something else — these things quite often do. And, of course, she was the person who found the body."

"I suppose," I said, "that would have been the most straightforward way to kill him. I mean, there wouldn't be any creeping around not wanting to be seen or anything."

"How long would you say it was between Rhys Hampden coming out and Lorna Spear going to see Dr. Morrison?"

"Oh, dear, I don't really know. It *seemed* like quite a long time, but it always does when you're waiting for something. Almost five minutes, perhaps, or a bit less. Anyway, old Mr. Prothero, who was his next patient, got fed up and went to complain and that's when Lorna went to see what the holdup was. Well, that's what we thought, of course.

140

But she could have gone in there, killed him and come back and said she'd found the body." I shook my head. "But could she? I mean, it would take an amazing nerve to do a thing like that. I don't know if Lorna could do that."

"If she was stalking Dr. Morrison," Roger said, "then she must be unbalanced in some way and when people are unbalanced they do peculiar things."

"I suppose so," I said doubtfully.

"I'll know a bit better when I've had a chance to talk to her."

"You'll mention the stalking?"

"It is pretty central to the investigation."

"But you won't say it was Nora — I mean, you won't say how you heard about it?"

"Of course not. 'Information received.' If she denies it and we find that she *was* connected with the murder, then your friend will have to give evidence."

"I'm sure she would be willing to do that. You said there were a couple of new leads. What is the other?"

"This mystery woman who visited Dr. Morrison — I think we must see if we can find her."

"Not easy."

"No. It's a pity your friend had scruples about watching her. Still there are other neighbors. Someone may have seen something useful."

"Poor Nora," I said, "she did want to protect John's privacy."

"If you get yourself murdered, then I'm afraid there is no such thing as privacy — everything has to come out and everything has to be examined. How else can we get to the bottom of things?"

"I know, and I'm sure Nora knows too — well, she must if she told you — but, all the same, she'll have felt she was betraying him. She was very protective of him."

"What was their relationship?" Roger asked casually.

"They were friends."

"Just friends?"

"Just friends. She was quite a bit older than him — though I know that doesn't seem to mean anything these days, but it would to Nora. No, he was her friend, and her father's friend too. John used to come down by himself when Nora was in London and go sailing with old Mr. Burton. I expect she told you that."

"Yes, I gathered they more or less made him one of the family."

"I think so. I do wish I'd known him like that, as a friend of Nora — I seem to have got him quite wrong."

"That doesn't sound like you, Sheila," Roger said, smiling. "I always count on your judgment of people."

"Like most people, I only ever saw him in his professional capacity — brilliant but disagreeable. Even my friend Alan, who always sang his praises as a doctor, never really saw the human being. I gather the other doctors didn't like him much — I don't think he socialized with any of them. Have you spoken to them yet?"

"Only briefly. I've read all the statements, but I wanted some sort of idea about their relationship with him before I asked directly about Dr. Morrison." He looked at me hopefully. "Have you heard anything?"

"Not really."

"Well, let me know if you do. I rely on you for all the gossip!" He looked at the kitchen clock. "Goodness, is that the time? I must be going. Thanks for the coffee, and remember, I look on you as my eyes and ears!"

"So can you do the scones and sandwiches?" Thea asked. "And if you *could* manage one of your chocolate cakes, they always go down very well."

"Oh, yes, that's all right if you won't need them till Saturday."

Now that Michael is captain of the local cricket team poor Thea has to organize the cricket teas.

"That's brilliant. Fiona's promised to make a sponge and some small cakes. It's such a blessing that she's going out with Phil Armstrong — she's a brilliant cook! So I think we should be all right."

"I do hope it's going to be dry," I said. "I suppose we should have expected a wet spell after all that fine weather."

"The forecast's not bad," Thea said absently. "Oh, there was one other thing I wanted to ask you. Alice is mad keen to come, but I don't think she'll last out the afternoon. Could you be an angel and take her back home with you after a bit?"

"I'd love to, but will you be all right with the teas?"

"Fiona said she'd give me a hand, and it would be such a help if you could see to Alice."

Saturday morning was overcast, but after a couple of hours the sun broke through and by the time I got down to the ground it was really quite pleasant.

"Just enough moisture in the air to help the ball swing a bit," Michael said, helping himself to one of the sandwiches I was putting out. "Let's hope we win the toss."

Alice, who was standing beside me, tugged at my skirt to attract my attention.

"Come to see Daddy play ball," she said. "Can Alice play ball?" she asked hopefully.

"Not just now, darling," I said. "Later on you can come home with Gran and we'll play ball."

Alice seemed satisfied with this promise and retreated to a corner of the pavilion, where she engaged in her current passion of dressing and undressing her baby doll and putting it into its carry-cot and taking it out again. When the match began I went outside and sat on one of the benches to watch. Michael's wish had not been granted and his side was put in to bat and lost two quick wickets.

"It looks as if Michael's going to have to play a captain's innings." Dr. Macdonald came and sat down beside me. "He and young Armstrong need to put on a decent number of runs to give our side any sort of chance."

"Oh, hello. Yes, you're right. Let's hope they both settle down."

We chatted for a while about the cricket and then I said, "I imagine you're still finding things difficult at the surgery."

"Badly understaffed," he said. "We've got this young Dutch chap — very good, we were lucky there — but he's just on a three months' contract and most of the people we've interviewed aren't suitable. We'd really like another woman, especially with Joanna off soon for goodness knows how long, but they're what everyone wants nowadays."

"I would have thought a Taviscombe practice might be attractive — sea, lovely countryside and all that. Ideal place to bring up a family."

"You'd think so, wouldn't you? But it doesn't seem to work like that. No, it's getting more and more difficult. That's why we thought we were so fortunate to get Morrison."

"Everyone says how brilliant he was."

"No question about that — though there was that business with Ken Webster. His son is still threatening to sue, which is absolute nonsense. He can't accept that the heart attack was quite different from the low-grade angina his father had had for years, and came right out of the blue. No one could have predicted that. I just hope his solicitor has the sense to advise him properly. . . . Oh, well-done — that has to be a six! Young Armstrong is shaping up really well."

"Mind if I join you?" Alan came and sat down with us on the bench. "I wanted to see this young man of Fiona's in action. He looks promising."

"I think he's got the makings of an opening bat," Alec Macdonald said, "and that's what we really need."

"So you don't think Richard Webster's got a case?" I asked, wanting to get the conversation back.

"No, not really, certainly not medically speaking."

"Richard Webster?" Alan said. "Is he still going on? I mean it was very sad about his father, but Richard seems obsessed and he's wound poor Moira up so she doesn't know *what's* happening."

"Perhaps after what's happened," I said, "Dr. Morrison dying like that, he may let things drop."

"I sincerely hope so," Alec Macdonald said. "I've enough on my plate as it is. Sheila, you know this policeman, Eliot. Have you any idea how the case is going?"

"I think they feel it's early days yet."

"He has only spoken briefly to my people. They all gave statements when it happened, but I think they expected to be questioned a bit more in depth."

"About how they got on with Dr. Morrison and things like that?" I asked.

"Something like that, certainly."

"How *did* they get on?" Alan asked.

"Well, you know how it is in any kind of closed community. There were tensions — only to be expected."

"I suppose," Alan said thoughtfully, "when you get someone like Morrison in general practice there's bound to be some jealousy. I believe he was doing some outside research."

"Yes. The trouble is, Sam Porter is doing research too, though his is for a drug company."

"So what caused the trouble?" Alan asked.

"Until Morrison arrived Sam had always been that member of the practice who was engaged in something special and important. It gave him a sort of status, I suppose — not to mention earning money for the practice. So when someone arrived who was, to put it bluntly, intellectually superior, who'd actually been at the cutting edge, as they say, of really high-powered research, well, you might say his nose was put out of joint."

"I can see that," Alan said. "It must have been awkward."

"Sam couldn't resist making snide remarks, trying to put Morrison down, but, of course, he wasn't in the same league. Morrison gave as good as he got, or ignored him in the sort of patronizing way that must have been very galling. What was even worse, he had quite a bit of expertise in the field that Sam was researching and I believe — though I never actually heard him do it — that he questioned some of Sam's findings."

"Oh, dear," I said. "I heard he didn't suffer fools gladly. Not," I added hastily, "that Dr. Porter is a fool, but I can see how impatient John Morrison might have been if he thought something hadn't been properly checked or clearly thought out."

Alec Macdonald sighed. "Too much of a perfectionist for his own good. I mean, wonderful academically, in the world of pure science, but in the real world, it can be uncomfortable for other people."

"And the others did find it uncomfortable?" Alan asked.

I was glad to hear Alan asking the questions I wanted the answers to. Alec Macdonald considered this for a moment. Then he said, "There were some more personal disagreements. Things happened that shouldn't have — I can't, obviously, go into details, but I was worried about the effect on the practice. We have to work as a team to some extent and when you get that sort of disharmony it throws the whole organization out of kilter. That's why I'm worried about this investigation — I honestly don't know what is going to come out. Everyone's on edge — not just the doctors, of course, but all the other staff — and since it seems possible that we may have a murderer in our midst, well, you can see how it is. Not to mention losing a man of Morrison's caliber in that appalling way."

We were all silent and it was almost a relief when there was a shout from the field and Phil Armstrong was out.

"Thirty-nine," Alan said, "not bad on this pitch."

"That chap of theirs is still getting the ball to swing a bit."

"The sun's quite hot. It might dry out later."

"Well, certainly, it would help, but it'll need more than that to help our spinners."

The talk then became exclusively of cricket, so I said good-bye and went back into the pavilion.

Thea was laying out cups and seeing to the tea urn.

"Oh, good," she said, "I was just coming to call you. I think Alice has had enough. She's starting to get a bit whiny. So if you could . . ."

"Of course." I went over to where Alice was moodily kicking the side of her doll's carry-cot. "Shall we take baby doll home and give her her tea?"

Tris and Foss, always glad of any diversion, came to greet us in the hall and Alice, her good humor restored, went off happily to throw a ball for Tris in the garden, while Foss watched disdainfully from a safe distance.

As I buttered the bread for the banana sandwiches and got out the iced fairy cakes, I thought about the conversation with Alec Macdonald. He was normally the most discreet of men, so he must have been exceptionally worried about the situation at the surgery to have spoken as freely as he did. Of course a murder does create fear and suspicion, especially where there's already been tension and mistrust, but I wondered what else — what he hadn't spoken of — might be disturbing him so much.

Chapter Eleven

"I really ought to check that everything's all right at John's house," Nora said. "I haven't been in there since — since he died, and I suppose someone ought to. It's just that — well, you know how it is — I can't quite bring myself to face it. I don't suppose . . ."

"You'd like me to come with you?"

"If you wouldn't mind."

"Of course I'll come. When?"

"Tomorrow if that's all right with you."

I don't really know what I expected John Morrison's house to be like — dour and forbidding, I suppose, full of large, dark furniture. But it wasn't like that at all.

"John always left his spare key with me," Nora said, letting us in. The house was not as large as Nora's, but like hers it was situated up a flight of steps, so that standing at the front door, you had a wonderful view of the bay. I followed her inside and stopped in surprise. Stepping through the front door, you found yourself in a big, open-plan area whose large windows flooded the room with light. The whole effect, indeed, was light and airy, white walls, modern furniture and thin, floating curtains. But somehow, it wasn't a feminine room. The furniture had strong, clean lines, for decoration there were large bronzes, and the pictures were vibrant and exciting. The whole room, though, focused on the windows. Through them you were constantly reminded of the sea outside, its changing moods and its unforgiving strength.

Nora looked at me and smiled. "Not quite what you expected?" she asked.

I shook my head. "Nothing like it," I said. "I'm amazed. It's really beautiful."

"John was a very creative person," Nora said. "He was imaginative in the way that some — a very few — scientists can be. He saw into the heart of things, if you know what I mean."

Looking around the room, I said, "I think I do."

Nora looked around. "It needs a good dusting," she said, "and I think I'd better air the place a bit." She moved over and opened the windows wide, letting in a fresh cool breeze and that unmistakable salt smell of sea air. I followed her through a door into the kitchen. Again, everything was well thought-out, with modern fittings and utensils.

"John enjoyed cooking," Nora said. "He was very good at it and he said it relaxed him."

We went back into the living area. "The study is upstairs," Nora said, and led the way up the polished open-tread wooden staircase to the upper floor. There were two rooms and a bathroom leading off the small landing. The study was the larger of the two rooms, at the front, looking out over the sea. The walls were lined with white-painted bookshelves, there was a modern desk with a computer and various files spread out, and a large table by the window housed a microscope and other scientific apparatuses. It was, in every sense of the word, a workroom, and because I knew its owner would no longer work there, it seemed particularly empty and desolate.

"He spent most of his time up here," Nora said, "working or just watching the sea."

She walked over to the window and I followed. Although it was a sunny day, there was a stiff breeze and the water was flecked with white. A small yacht was tacking towards the harbor, its sail keeling over as it came about. Standing there in that room, looking at that view, I felt for the first time I knew something of the sort of person John Morrison must have been and I understood just a little the immense loss Nora must be feeling.

As I turned away from the window I noticed a photograph on the desk. Three young people in their early twenties. Two young men on either side of a girl, with their arms around each other, all bright, eager, full of life — John Morrison, Virginia, and Francis Wheeler. Nora's glance followed mine.

"Yes, that was taken when they were at medical school together. They were very close in those days. Actually Francis and John were friends first, and although Francis was very keen on Virginia himself, they remained friends for a long time after the marriage."

"But not to the end?"

"No," she said, "by the time Virginia went off with the man Sutton, Francis had gone to work in America." She paused. "But there'd been a breakup between them before that. Something happened — John said, something unforgivable. He wouldn't say what it was, but it obviously upset him too much to talk to me about it."

"Goodness. And how strange to think that they both ended up in the West Country. They must have come across each other at the hospital. After all Francis Wheeler comes down every fortnight to hold clinics there. Did John ever say anything about seeing him?"

Nora shook her head. "No, never. I must say I was surprised to see Francis at the funeral." She picked up the photograph. "It was odd seeing him with Virginia."

"Rekindling old fires?" I asked.

Nora laughed. "Oh, no. Francis, I'm sure, isn't going to risk his marriage to a young, rich wife with a useful father — she's the only daughter of a fashionable London consultant. No, I can't imagine why he was there." She replaced the photograph on the desk. "Oh, well, we'd better get on."

John Morrison's bedroom, at the back of the house, overlooking a small walled garden, was, in contrast with the rest of the house, unremarkable. Plain walls, no pictures, the minimum of furniture — a wardrobe, a chest of drawers, a double bed and a bedside table with a leather-bound book on it. Curious, I picked it up and said, "It's a Bible."

We looked at each other. "There's something marking a place," I said, and opened the book. It opened at the Epistles and my eye was caught by a penciled line in the margin: " 'Be not deceived; God is not mocked: for whatsoever a man soweth, that shall he also reap,' " I read. "Saint Paul to the Galatians. A son of the manse, you said?"

Nora nodded. "But I'd no idea he read the Bible." I handed it to her and she read the passage. "I wonder what all that was about and who he meant." She closed the book and replaced it on the bedside table.

" 'There's a great text in Galatians' . . . something, something . . . 'it entails / Twenty-nine distinct damnations, each certain if the other fails.' "

Nora looked at me in surprise.

"Browning," I said, "but I can't remember it properly. Oh, the awfulness of English literature — it leaves you with half-remembered tags, not even really relevant, but lying there ready to be triggered off!"

Nora looked down at the piece of paper in her hand. "Oh, bother, I've lost the place." She opened the Bible and leafed through it. "Does Galatians come before or after Ephesians? Oh, there it is. Good heavens!"

She handed me the piece of paper that had marked the passage. It was a short note scribbled in pencil on a sheet torn from some sort of small pad. It simply said,

I've got to see you — I can't bear this. Text me. PLEASE. J.

157

We looked at each other and Nora said, "J. or Jay? What was going on?"

"It sounds rather desperate," I said. "That underlining scored right through the paper. And why would he keep it in his Bible?"

Nora shook her head. "I don't understand. He never said anything. . . ." Her voice trailed away. "He had a way of keeping difficult things to himself, but he usually told me about them in the end. Now," she said sadly, "he never will."

"Do you feel like coming to look at a garden?" Rosemary asked.

I looked at her inquiringly.

"The wife of one of Jack's clients is opening her garden to the public for some good cause or other and I rather feel I ought to go."

"Where is it and when?" I asked cautiously.

"On Saturday and this side of Tiverton. The forecast's good and it'll be a nice drive along the Exe Valley."

"Yes, all right, I'd quite like to."

The garden was, in fact, very nice, beautifully laid out and a riot of color. Though the owner, who greeted Rosemary effusively, was full of lamentations.

"It's *not* what it should be — all that dreadful hot weather played absolute *havoc* and we were watering until all hours!"

"It looks lovely," I said.

"Absolutely gorgeous," Rosemary added.

"*So* kind, but I do wish you could have seen it last month. . . ." She drifted away.

Rosemary and I looked at each other and laughed.

"Pure Ruth Draper!" I said. "It does seem to be a timeless and universal thing!"

"The roses are gorgeous. Just look at that Peace over there — the flowers are as big as cabbages — and the clematis! So unfair, my clematis just puts out one miserable flower at a time. How *does* one manage to get all the flowers to come out at once?"

We were wandering around the garden admiring the flowers and shrubs when Rosemary clutched my arm.

"Look," she said, "there's Janet Dobson with Lorna. Let's go along this path and avoid them — I really can't be doing with that woman."

We edged behind some bushes and made our way to the lawn, where tables had been set out and teas ("Cream £2.50; Plain £1.75") were being served.

"Are you going to have a cream or a plain?" Rosemary asked.

"Oh, plain, I think. I had rather a large lunch."

"It seems to be self-service," Rosemary said, indicating the trestle table where two flustered women in aprons (obviously friends of the owner of the garden and roped in to help) were trying to pour milk and tea, juggle cakes and give change simultaneously. We chose our cakes and took our cups of tea and I tried to pay for them both, which caused an agony of arithmetic on the part of the larger lady.

"Both together, is it? Yes, well, if you can give me the four pence, then I can give you a pound, because I don't seem to have any fifty-pence coins. Oh, thank you so much, if you're sure — it *is* for a good cause after all!"

"I think you were wise to have the coffee sponge," Rosemary said when we had settled down at one of the few free tables. "This flapjack's a bit chewy."

"Do you mind if we join you?" Janet Dobson had come up behind us with a tray in her hand. "I thought I saw you earlier — I said to Lorna, 'I do believe that's Rosemary and Sheila, quite a coincidence.' "

Rosemary muttered something that might be taken for assent and I moved the other two chairs so that they could sit down.

"They've got a good crowd here," Janet went on. "Of course we all like looking round other people's gardens." She laughed. "You can't help being curious, can you?"

Lorna sat there looking morose and contributing nothing to the conversation.

Janet turned to her daughter. "Lorna, dear, would you go and get me some sugar — I thought there'd be some on the table. Isn't it awful? I know I should give up sugar in my tea, but I've never been able to manage it."

Lorna got up and moved slowly away towards the trestle tables. Janet leaned forward and spoke confidentially. "I thought it might take her out of herself having a little trip out. She's been really bad ever since — you know, the *murder*."

"It must have been a dreadful shock for her," I said, "finding Dr. Morrison like that."

"Oh, yes." Janet spoke almost enthusiastically, obviously enjoying the drama of it all, "a terrible shock. She hasn't been right since. I made her come and stay with me of course — it wasn't fit for her to be on her own, and she's been off work. In fact" — she leaned forward — "I wouldn't be surprised if she quits for good. Traumatized, that's what Dr. Macdonald says she is. He's given

161

her sedatives and so on, but I don't think she'll ever get over it."

"How dreadful," I said. "Dr. Morrison wasn't a popular man, but I can't think why anyone should have wanted to kill him."

"He was," Janet said, looking over her shoulder as if afraid of being overheard, "a bit of a ladies' man, so I've heard."

"Really?" I asked. "I'd never have guessed it. He didn't look the type."

"Oh, yes, a real dark horse. Lorna said he'd even made a pass at her — that was some time ago."

"Good heavens!"

Lorna's return with a bowl of sugar put an end to Janet's confidences and Rosemary, who had taken no part in this conversation, said, "We really ought to go now. I have to be back by five," and we made our escape.

In the car going home, Rosemary said, "That woman! Positively reveling in it all. And what was all that nonsense about Dr. Morrison making a pass at Lorna — as if he would, well, not at *her!*"

I told Rosemary about the stalking business. "So you see," I said, "she's obviously been fantasizing about the whole thing — it's all a bit sinister."

"It certainly is. I always thought there was something peculiar about that girl. How awful for Dr. Morrison. It must have been awkward, working together like that."

"Perhaps," I said, "he had it out with her and that tipped her over the edge and she killed him."

Rosemary cautiously overtook a large tractor and trailer parked on a bend. "Well, you do hear of such things, though perhaps only in films and the more sensational Sunday papers. Still, that doesn't mean it couldn't happen in Taviscombe."

"As far as I can see," I said, "it's more of a motive for murder than anything else I've heard of."

"She did look awful," Rosemary said, "sort of haunted, if that's the word I want."

"I know what you mean," I agreed. "Her mind was obviously somewhere else. She's always been a bit sullen, but it was different today. She really didn't seem to be with us."

"Of course, it can't help to have Janet Dobson for a mother, especially if you've got something on your mind. Can you imagine confiding in her!"

"In a way you have to feel sorry for her, Lorna, I mean, being obsessed by something or someone — it must consume you, color your whole life. I suppose it must have been like that for Lorna, and now he's gone (whether she was the one who killed him or not) she must have a terrible emptiness. No wonder she's acting oddly — her whole world must have been wrenched out of focus."

"Well," Rosemary said robustly, "I don't want to be unfeeling, but I, for one, will be quite glad if she leaves the practice — I mean, we don't want anyone mentally unbalanced arranging the appointments!"

When I got back I was still thinking of Lorna, turning over in my mind what Nora had told me about her hanging about outside John Morrison's house. Even if he'd made a joke of it to Nora, it must still have been worrying to know that a disturbed person (and she must surely be clinically disturbed) was stalking him. I wondered if he had told any of the other doctors about it — as a case study, perhaps, not naming names — if, indeed, anyone else apart from Nora knew about it.

Then there was Janet's description of him as "a ladies' man." Had she been describing him like that from what Lorna had said, or was there other talk about him, at the surgery perhaps? Did anyone else know about Jay? What had happened there? The note in the Bible seemed to indicate that that particular relationship was over, ended, apparently by him. "I can't bear this" sounded

164

desperate. Had Jay been superseded by someone else? If so, who? The questions seemed endless and I hadn't the faintest idea where to find the answers.

My thoughts were interrupted by a loud cry. Foss wished to tell me that he had come in, and wasn't it time some food was forthcoming? But when we got into the kitchen I remembered that I'd meant to cook his fish before I went out, but I'd left in a hurry and forgotten it.

"Oh, Foss, I'm sorry. If you want something now, you'll just have to have dried food or a tin."

I opened a tin for each of the animals and put their plates down. Foss sniffed suspiciously at his and looked up at me incredulously. "That's all there is," I said firmly. Tris, happy with any food, had already demolished his plateful and stood, his head on one side, watching hopefully, as Foss picked reluctantly at his food. Tris knew from experience that if he waited patiently, he could clear up the remains that Foss had left as a protest.

I was standing smiling at the little scene played out, almost as a ritual, every few days, when the telephone rang. It was Nora.

"Sheila." She sounded breathless and

upset. "Do you think I could come round? Something very peculiar's happened and I'd like to talk to you about it."

Chapter Twelve

When Nora arrived she seemed much more calm and collected.

"Come in and sit down," I said. "What will you have? Sherry or gin and tonic?"

"Oh, gin and tonic, please. Sheila, I'm sorry to break in on your evening like this. I do hope I'm not messing up your plans. But the thing is, I've had a bit of a shock and I really wanted to talk to someone about it."

"That's fine. No plans at all. Just me and the telly. So what's happened?"

Nora paused for a moment as if to gather her thoughts. "You know I told you that John's solicitor was in London. Maurice Seaton. He's my solicitor too — in fact he's a friend as well as a solicitor. John and I have known him for ages — he's really nice. Anyway, I had a letter from him today saying that since I was a close friend of John's, he thought I ought to know what was in his will, so he enclosed a photocopy."

"Yes?"

"There were a couple of bequests to medical charities and a few things he left to me — some of his bronzes and pictures that he knew I liked, and the boat, because it had originally been my father's. And he asked me to go through his papers and destroy anything I felt he would wish me to."

Nora put her glass down and leaned forward. "John was really very comfortably off. He lived quite frugally — his only extravagances were books and the boat. And with property prices as they are, I expect his house will fetch a fair amount."

"Sure to," I said, "especially in that position overlooking the bay."

"So you see, there's quite a lot of money involved."

"Are there any relatives?"

"Only some sort of cousin he hasn't seen for years."

"So?"

"He's left the lot to Joanna Stevenson."

"What!"

"Joanna. Jay. J."

"Good heavens! So she was the woman . . . and you never suspected — he never mentioned her?"

"He may have done in passing, along with the other doctors in the practice, but no, never — never in any other way."

168

A thought struck me. "And she's pregnant."

"Exactly."

"You think it's John's child?"

"That would explain the money."

We were both silent for a while. Then I said, "But the note in the Bible. It sounds as if he'd ended it. Would he have done that if he'd known about the child?"

"That may have been why he did."

"What on earth do you mean?"

"John never wanted children. He had this extraordinary idea that he'd be a bad father."

"But why?"

"His own father was a very difficult man, strict, dominant, controlling — a caricature of an old-fashioned stern Presbyterian minister. He made John's childhood thoroughly miserable. He was the only child, so he got the full force of all his father's theories and prejudices."

"What about his mother?"

"She died when John was very young — they had a succession of grim housekeepers."

"How ghastly. But still, that wouldn't mean that John would be the same."

"You probably know that John was deeply interested in genetics — he'd done research, was continuing to do so here. It wasn't just his father. His paternal grandfather was much the same — John felt that explained his father's character — and there was, apparently, a history of actual violence in the family."

"But surely, that doesn't necessarily mean . . ."

"Some specialists," Nora said, "who've been deeply involved with a particular theory over a long period of time can end up seeing what they want to see."

"But that's terrible."

"I tried to argue with him once or twice, but I was never going to get anywhere, so I gave up."

"Do you think that was why he and Virginia split up?"

"I think that was part of it. I believe he discussed it with her before they got married. But she said it didn't matter. Well, she was young and she had her career — she was ambitious."

"But?"

"But as time went on, I suppose it began to get to her. She knew that John would never change his mind. She and Sutton have two children."

"Oh, dear, what a mess! Do you think Clive Stevenson knows?"

"About John and Joanna? I'm not sure."

"Actually," I said, remembering something, "I think he probably does."

I told her about the little scene I'd witnessed in the corridor at the practice.

"There was something about the way she pulled her arm away when he tried to talk to her, as if she'd already distanced herself and didn't want anything to do with him."

"So," Nora said thoughtfully, "if he knew about the affair, he'd have had his suspicions about the baby."

"Which," I said, "gives him a pretty strong motive for murder."

"True," Nora agreed. "But then," she continued, "so had Joanna."

"What?"

"Just think about it. She had been rejected — and in the most painful way possible, because she was going to have John's child. Just think how that would have made her feel. He may even have asked her to have an abortion."

"How terrible. But look," I went on, "if John had broken things off with her, why did he leave her money in his will? I mean, he didn't know that he was going to die."

"I expect that was John being extra cautious," Nora said. "He'd have wanted to provide for the child financially and since he

171

was that much older than Joanna, it would be likely that he would die first, so he would want to make sure that the money would go on coming to her after his death."

"It all sounds so cold-blooded, so impersonal."

"No, I don't think he meant it like that. But the fact is that John was a logical person, who tackled each situation as if it was a problem that could be solved by rational thinking."

"That sounds cold-blooded to me," I said.

Nora smiled. "He was a very complex person. He lived his own life on an intellectual level, as it were, but he was capable of great warmth and sympathy. He was wonderful to me when Father died."

"But not," I pointed out, "to poor Joanna!"

"In that case, I think his overwhelming fear of fatherhood was stronger than anything else. It really was something of an obsession with him, and you know how it is with obsessions — they obliterate everything else."

We were both silent for a while, trying, I suppose, to take in the implications of what had happened. Then Nora said, "I don't know what to do. I really don't."

"You ought, really," I said slowly, "to tell the police. I mean, there are these new motives for John's death, motives they have no way of knowing about, well, not unless you tell them."

Nora shook her head. "But how can I? It would be the worst kind of betrayal of John."

"No," I said firmly, "*not* the worst kind — that would be allowing his murderer to get away with it. You owe it to John, you must see that."

"I suppose so," she said reluctantly. "But if that's so, why do I feel so awful about telling them?"

"Your John was a very private person," I said, "and you feel you're destroying his privacy. But there's nothing private about murder. You *must* tell Roger. Even when they find out about Joanna and the baby and the money (and they will very soon), they still need to know how he felt about the baby — there's no way they could guess that. Only you or Joanna can tell them, and I doubt if she will."

"You're right, of course, and yes, I'll do it. I'll ring Roger Eliot tomorrow. Somehow I won't mind so much telling him. It's not a situation that everyone would understand, but I think he will."

"I'm sure he will. I know you're doing the right thing. I wonder," I said "what Joanna will do now — will she leave her husband? For that matter would he have her back?"

"I suppose, before the baby, she may have thought she'd move in with John."

"Would he have wanted that?"

Nora shook her head. "I doubt it. After Virginia he always avoided any sort of real commitment."

"You sound as if there've been others, before Joanna."

"There were a few, but he was — how shall I put it? — very wary after Virginia. I don't think he ever recovered after that."

"That's sad. Your John was certainly a complicated character."

"Complex — yes. That's what made him so interesting. I'd never met anyone like him, and now I don't suppose I ever will again." She sighed and looked at her watch. "Goodness, is that the time? I must be going."

"No, do stay and have supper — it's only pasta, but I've made the sauce, so it won't take a minute. Come into the kitchen and talk to me while I get it together."

It really is extraordinary how things multiply — inanimate things, books, flower vases (I must have at least twenty, none of which I can remember actually buying) and, especially, magazines. It doesn't seem to me, when I try to consider it rationally, that I buy many of them, very few on a regular basis, usually on an impulse or when I'm going on a train journey, but there they all are — copies of *The Spectator, Gardening World, The New Yorker, Good Housekeeping, Country Life,* not to mention all the color supplements — forming unsteady piles on small tables or cluttering up valuable work space on the kitchen dresser. Kept because there's always *one* article that I didn't get around to reading, or something I wanted to show Michael or Thea, or a specially interesting recipe that I meant to cut out and never did, all kept, I must confess, because throwing things away is something I'm always going to do tomorrow.

When once again I knocked a pile of the wretched things onto the floor in the sitting room, I decided something had to be done. I gathered together as many as I could manage, stuffed them into a large canvas bag, put them into the car and drove down to the outpatient department of the hospital.

Lyn Varley, an old hospital acquaintance, was in reception, though the waiting room was empty.

"Hello, Lyn," I said, "can you use some magazines for the waiting room? I can never quite bring myself to throw them out and I thought you might be glad of them."

"That's brilliant," Lyn said enthusiastically. "They get so chewed up and mangled here and people tear recipes and things out of them — sometimes there's only a cover left. They'll be *very* welcome!" She emerged from behind her glass partition and helped me to take them out of the bag. "What a lovely lot — there's several here I might just borrow to read myself before I put them out!"

I looked around the empty waiting room. "No clinic this morning?" I asked.

"No, nothing on Wednesdays until one forty-five. That's Mr. Wheeler's."

"Does he come every Wednesday?"

"Oh, no, just the first Wednesday in the month."

"Oh, right. And he came last month?"

She looked at me curiously. "Yes. Why?"

"Oh, no reason, I just wondered if the police came to tell him about poor Dr. Morrison. They were old friends, apparently."

"Not as far as I know. Mind you, he was late for his clinic that day. He said he had a puncture and it took ages to get it changed, especially with all the traffic on the road."

"The holiday traffic's awful, worse than ever this year," I said. "It took me ages just to get to Williton the other day. Have you been away yet?"

"No, Derek and I usually go somewhere warm abroad in January — I think a break does you more good then, don't you?"

As I left the hospital I passed Clive Stevenson, presumably on duty there. I would have said hello, but it was perfectly obvious that he was miles away, lost in goodness only knows what thoughts.

As I drove home, I considered the fact that Francis Wheeler *had* been in Taviscombe the day John Morrison was killed. And he'd been late for his clinic. I wondered how familiar he was with the layout of the surgery. It was more than likely he'd been there sometimes to talk to Alec Macdonald or Sam Porter, both of whom were interested in orthopedics. I remembered what Nora had told me about the awful thing that John said Francis Wheeler had done. I wondered how I could find out what it was and if it was terrible enough to be the motive for a murder.

Rosemary phoned the following day.

"Sheila, I have an immense favor to ask you."

"Something to do with your mother?" I asked.

"How did you guess! No, actually, I promised to take her to the chiropodist this afternoon, but I've got to look after the children. Roger's had to go up to London on business of some kind and Jilly's suddenly decided to travel up with him so that she can see an old school friend who's over from South Africa. I'm sorry to spring it on you like this, but it's all been a bit short notice. I'll quite understand if you've made other arrangements. I mean, I *could* take Delia and Alex with me — the appointment's at four o'clock — but you know what Mother's like with them, always criticizing!"

"No, that's fine," I said. "I can easily manage four o'clock. Anyway, it's been ages since I've seen her — I've been feeling guilty about that."

"Mother's very good," Rosemary said morosely, "at making people feel guilty. Well, if you're sure you don't mind . . ."

I wondered what "business" Roger had in London, and if it had anything to do with John Morrison's murder. He might have decided to talk to people at the hospital who used to know him — I didn't know if he'd already spoken to Virginia. I wondered too if Nora had had a chance to speak to him

178

about Joanna and Clive. The more I thought about it, the more it seemed to me that a lot of people might have had a reason for wanting John Morrison dead.

It was funny, I thought as I began collecting things from the linen basket to take downstairs, how much my view of him had changed. All the things Nora had told me made me realize what an unusual and interesting person he must have been, and I regretted never having had the chance to get to know him. More than ever I could see what a gap he'd have left in Nora's life. She too was a reserved person, not making friends easily — I was an exception because we'd grown up together. As far as I knew she'd never had any serious romantic relationship (or if she had, she'd never told me about it) and this friendship with John, someone with what she considered such fine qualities, seemed to have been the most important thing in her life. And on his part, he would probably (from what I knew about him now) have valued the things that Nora could offer him: the intellectual rigor, the calm and rational examination of any problem, together with a warm but undemanding affection. It had been, it occurred to me, that rare thing nowadays, a perfect friendship between a man and a woman.

I gathered up the clothes and bed linen and went to make my way downstairs. I was brought to a halt by Foss, who suddenly greeted me with loud cries when I was halfway down the staircase. He has this habit of coming to find me when he's been out, and loudly announcing his safe arrival home, something I usually find rather touching, but on this occasion the sudden unexpected noise made me drop my armful of washing.

"Oh, Foss! Now look what you've made me do!"

Tris, attracted by the commotion, came into the hall barking and by the time I'd gathered up the scattered garments, got them into the washing machine and placated my two vociferous friends with food, I was obliged to go and get myself ready to collect Mrs. Dudley. This was no easy task, since I knew that whatever I chose to wear would be subjected to the silent but critical scrutiny that had been successfully undermining my confidence ever since I was seven years old.

Chapter Thirteen

I arrived at Mrs. Dudley's, as I always do, a good ten minutes before the appointed time, but she was already sitting in her chair by the window, wearing her hat and coat and an expression of patient resignation, as of one who has been waiting a *very* long time. Mrs. Dudley is now the only person I know who regularly wears a hat and today's was a navy blue straw with a brisk petersham ribbon bow at the back.

"Ah, there you are, Sheila," she said, glancing pointedly at the clock. "I am quite ready."

As we drove to the chiropodist she said, "Since we are a little early, perhaps you would be kind enough to stop at Morgan's. I want to leave a pair of spectacles to be adjusted."

Mrs. Dudley is always doing this, popping in little extra tasks apparently casually, although the whole thing is carefully planned, and I have come to expect it. "Why doesn't she just *say* what she wants to do?" I once asked Rosemary. "The simple exercise of power," Rosemary explained, "is not enough; she likes to add just one more thing to top up the pressure."

Needless to say there wasn't anywhere to park outside the optician's and I had to stop in the space reserved for taxis, which provoked sour glances from the drivers. However, when they saw who it was being helped out of the car, their looks turned to pity rather than wrath, since they had all of them suffered at one time or another from Mrs. Dudley's forceful personality.

When we finally got to the chiropodist we were five minutes late.

"I am so sorry we are late," Mrs. Dudley said to Lisa, the receptionist. "Transport difficulties, so tiresome," and she swept past her into the surgery.

"That's you told," Lisa said, smiling.

Since when I was with Mrs. Dudley, I didn't dare go away and come back, I settled down to have a nice chat with Lisa. She has an extensive family and my inquiries about them and her answers usually took up most of the half hour of Mrs. Dudley's appointment. We had covered her sister in New Zealand and her sister's husband, and the eldest boy in Tasmania, and gradually worked round (by way of her husband's brother in Carlisle) to relatives living in Taviscombe. Her eldest son, now at university in Bath, was doing well, her daughter who had just taken her A levels was anxiously awaiting her results, but her youngest son, Graham, hadn't been at all well.

"It was chicken pox," she said, "and he had it really badly. Poor little soul, he was in a terrible state — there was a swimming competition he was supposed to be in at school, but of course that was quite out of the question. I rang up the surgery and they said, 'Can you bring him in?' But I said no, his temperature was right up and I didn't want to risk it. I mean, even if I wrapped him up in a blanket, there'd be all that time in the waiting room! Well, fortunately it was that nice receptionist — Valerie, isn't it? — and she said she'd see what she could do and then she said Dr. Porter had just come in and since he didn't have a surgery, he'd be round straightaway."

"Goodness," I said, "you *were* lucky to get a house call!"

"Well," Lisa said, "I didn't know how lucky until the next day when I heard about Dr. Morrison."

"You mean . . . ?"

"It must have been just about the time

poor Dr. Morrison was killed that Dr. Porter came to see Graham."

I looked at her inquiringly.

"Well, if it had been any later — after the murder — I don't suppose any of them would have been available to call — helping the police with their inquiries, or whatever they call it."

"No, I suppose they wouldn't have," I said thoughtfully.

"It was a dreadful thing," Lisa said, "and in the surgery too — it makes you feel nowhere is safe, doesn't it?"

"Absolutely. But how is Graham now?"

"Oh, he's quite all right now. Amazing, isn't it, how they can be down one moment and right up the next!"

When I took Mrs. Dudley home she said, "You'll stay to tea, Sheila."

Since this was more a command than an inquiry, I said that of course I'd love to. Actually, by then I felt the need for a cup of tea. The small tea table, already spread with a white crochet-edged cloth, stood beside the small fire (lit even in the summer) in the sitting room. Elsie, Mrs. Dudley's devoted maid, came bustling in with the silver teapot and put it down beside the fine Royal Worcester china and the splendid array of sandwiches and cakes. I found it extraordinary, but somehow comforting, to think that even in the twenty-first century this little ritual took place every day whether Mrs. Dudley had visitors or not.

"Will you pour, please, Sheila," she said, and continued sharply, "and don't forget to warm the teacups. The hot-water jug is to your left."

When I had successfully negotiated the tea pouring (almost as complicated in its way, I felt, as the Japanese version) and handed Mrs. Dudley the cucumber sandwiches, she settled herself in her high-backed chair and began to cross-question me about any local gossip I might have accumulated. Unfortunately, since I hadn't known in advance that I was going to see her, I was woefully ill prepared and realized that the meager information I was able to give her was proving unsatisfactory. She interrupted my version of Lisa's news about her sister in Auckland.

"Yes, yes, I know all about that." She leaned forward. "Now tell me all about this business with Dr. Morrison. I believe you were actually there when it happened."

"Well, yes, I was — at least I was in the waiting room, but I didn't really see anything."

"Don't be ridiculous, Sheila. You have

eyes in your head — you must have seen something."

I gave her an account, as far as I could remember it, of what had happened that morning. "Of course," I concluded, "they didn't say Dr. Morrison had been killed. They just said there'd been an accident."

"Dr. Macdonald was there, you say?"

"Yes, he was the other doctor on duty."

"Well, I shouldn't think *he* was too sorry to see the back of Dr. Morrison."

"You surely don't think —"

"Of course not," she replied impatiently. "I've known Alec Macdonald since he was a child. No, what I was about to say when you interrupted was that I heard that there was some sort of disagreement between them. Have you heard anything about that?" she demanded. I shook my head and she continued. "Personally I think it is a great loss. Dr. Morrison was a distinguished doctor with the highest qualifications and the practice was very lucky to have him."

I looked at her in surprise. Mrs. Dudley's approval was not given lightly.

"Did you know him, then?" I asked.

"I did see him on two occasions when Alec Macdonald was away on some sort of *course*." The word was spoken with some disdain. "I know Dr. Morrison was not popular in the town, but I always speak as I find, and he was most civil to me."

I gave him full marks for recognizing and appreciating Mrs. Dudley's energy and spirit.

"He was a very brilliant man," I said, "with many excellent qualities."

"Precisely," Mrs. Dudley said approvingly, "which is why I was surprised that Alec Macdonald said that he regretted taking him on."

"Really? How did you hear that?"

"Mavis Carpenter overheard him speaking to Dr. Howard about it. She was waiting for her X-ray at the hospital and they were standing there talking. Of course they didn't see her. She was round the corner in that little annex place — you know where I mean — but she heard them quite clearly."

"What did Dr. Macdonald say?"

"He said that if he'd known the trouble Dr. Morrison would cause, he would never have taken him on."

"Did he say what sort of trouble?"

"No, they moved away and Mavis," Mrs Dudley spoke impatiently, "didn't hear any more."

I suddenly remembered the snatch of conversation *I* had heard at the hospital when Alec Macdonald told Dr. Howard that he'd spoken to someone strongly and that it was the last thing the practice needed. That must surely have referred to Dr. Morrison and been about his relationship with Joanna Stevenson. I was brought up sharp by Mrs. Dudley.

"Do *you* know anything about this, Sheila?"

I pulled myself together quickly. "No, no, I don't."

She regarded me suspiciously and I tried to assume an expression of bland innocence, though I knew from long experience how difficult it was to hide anything from her.

"Well," she said in a dissatisfied tone, "there was obviously something going on."

"Perhaps it was something to do with Kenneth Webster," I suggested. "You know his son's been threatening to sue Dr. Morrison over his father's death."

"Absolute rubbish!" Mrs. Dudley said vehemently. "Everyone knows that Kenneth Webster has been at death's door for years. I'm surprised they were able to keep him alive as long as they did. Richard Webster's always been very *grasping* — I suppose he thinks he can get some sort of money out of all this."

"He says his mother's been very distressed by it all."

"Anyone," Mrs. Dudley said magisterially, "would be distressed if they had a fool like Richard Webster for a son." She looked at me sharply. "You don't imagine that Richard Webster had anything to do with Dr. Morrison's death?"

"Well . . ."

"Quite impossible. For one thing he may be full of bluster, but like all bullies, he's a coward underneath. He didn't even have the nerve to stand up to Dr. Morrison face-to-face, only blackguard him behind his back. Besides, he was in the Isle of Wight when it happened."

"Really?"

"He took his mother to see her sister Evelyn in Shanklin, though what she wanted to do that for, I can't imagine — they've never got on ever since Evelyn married that insurance salesman. Still, I suppose it made a change for her after Kenneth died."

She passed over her cup for me to refill it. "No, as I said," she continued, "Richard thought he might get some money out of his father's death. It's this dreadful compensation culture. People nowadays seem unwilling to take any responsibility for their own actions. I saw in the *Daily Telegraph*

189

only the other day that there are lawyers who make a living out of claiming compensation for people tripping over paving stones and other such nonsense. I cannot think what this country's coming to!"

I passed her the plate with the chocolate éclairs in the hope of diverting her from the enormities of modern life, a subject she was capable of enlarging on ad infinitum.

"Thank you, Sheila, perhaps just the one. Dr. Macdonald says I need to keep my strength up."

I didn't imagine he had actually specified cream cakes for this purpose, but I was glad to find a way of getting the conversation back to medical matters.

"They're finding it a bit of a strain at the surgery," I said, "being so short-staffed now that they don't have Dr. Morrison. It's more difficult than ever to get an appointment. A lot of people settle for seeing Nancy — we're very lucky to have such a good nurse-practitioner."

"That is no way to run a practice," Mrs. Dudley said severely. "I wouldn't dream of seeing anyone but a proper doctor. I believe Nancy Williams is an excellent girl — her grandmother was a friend of mine — but that is not the same thing at all. Of course Dr. Macdonald visits me at home — one of those girls in reception was impertinent enough to suggest that I should go to the surgery, but I soon put a stop to that! I did see one of the nurses once," she continued, "and she said that at my age I should have my main meal at lunchtime and not in the evening."

"Really?"

Mrs Dudley nodded. "Of course I put her in her place," she said. "I told her that I did not imagine that the Queen had her main meal at midday and even the most rabid republican could hardly claim that Her Majesty was not in robust health *at her age!*"

When I got back home I was (as I always am after playing lady-in-waiting to Mrs. Dudley) absolutely exhausted. Having had such a large tea, I had no wish even to think about supper (though like Mrs. Dudley and the Queen I have my main meal in the evening), so I poured myself a large gin and tonic, and flopped down on the sofa. But I wasn't able to relax for very long, since the animals, having had a run about outside when I got back, now demanded to be let in and fed. Mechanically I got their food out of the fridge, warmed it up in the microwave, put it down for them and was just about to go back to my glass and my sofa when the phone rang.

Just for a moment I contemplated letting it ring, but I never can, so I reluctantly went over to answer it.

"Sheila, I'm really sorry to bother you again like this." It was Nora. "Something's come up and I'd really like to talk to you about it."

"Of course. Do come round."

"No, I won't disturb your evening again, and anyway, I'd like to think about it a bit more before I speak to you. Would tomorrow morning be all right?"

"Yes, that's fine. I'm in all morning."

"About eleven, then, if that suits you. Thank you so much."

I put the phone down feeling more disturbed in a way than if Nora had actually come round. Now I would spend the evening wondering what on earth she wanted to tell me — something important, obviously, but what? It was very frustrating. I finished my drink and poured myself another one. I put on the television but couldn't concentrate. Even my favorite soap didn't hold my attention, nor a documentary about ancient Egypt. I must have drifted off to sleep because I woke with a start to find it was ten thirty and the screen was filled with depressing images of various world trouble spots.

Foss, who has a very accurate internal clock, was pacing up and down the room declaring loudly that it was time to switch off the television and prepare for bed. As I got my tray ready for the morning he sat bolt upright on the microwave, looking (perhaps influenced by the television program) particularly Egyptian — rather like the reproduction figure I had from the British Museum. He gave me a disdainful stare as if to remind me that he was a Temple Cat and that *his* ancestors were Sacred. Tris, who was more interested in supper, contented himself with giving anxious little whines in case I had forgotten the priorities.

As I went upstairs my mind went back to Nora's call. Presumably it was something about John Morrison. It was borne in on me what an important part of her life he had been and how empty it must seem to her now. It had been an unusual relationship — unusual for these days, certainly, though I could think of a few parallels in literature. I could see how they must have responded to each other — two rare spirits. The fact that John had been close to her father was important to her, and after he died, she must have felt that John was all the family she had, or, indeed, was likely to have.

She had made him her life, not really seeking out her old friends (thinking about it, I realized that I hadn't seen her very often since her return) or making new ones. And now that he'd gone, and in such tragic circumstances, she was using all the incidents surrounding the investigation into his death to cling to him, so that she could feel that something of him still remained. Perhaps she would never be able to start her life again until the whole business of his death had been settled, and unless something dramatic happened to bring the investigation to a conclusion, I didn't think that was very likely in the near future. I felt that I must do what I could to hasten that conclusion for Nora's sake if for nothing else.

Certainly I now knew that Dr. Porter had an alibi as had Alec Macdonald and the girls (apart from Lorna) in reception, but I had no idea about any of the others. Obviously Roger would know who had an alibi and who hadn't and I made a resolution to try and find out what he knew.

I switched on the radio beside my bed hoping for a reading from *The Book at Bedtime,* but it was on the wrong station and I got what appeared to be a phone-in about football.

"Yes, Dave," a Northern voice was saying with some force, "I'm on my mobile in the car on our way back from the match. Yeah, we was rubbish, absolute rubbish! What that team needs is a bitta metal, a bitta grit —"

"Thanks, Trev," another voice interrupted him, "that's all we have time for. Remember, all of you, keep on with the texts and e-mails and don't forget our Rant Line's open twenty-four hours a day, seven days a week, so let's have *your* thoughts. . . ."

Aware of my inadequacy at understanding one of many aspects of the present day, I switched off the radio and opened *The Last Chronicle of Barset*, sinking back with some relief into a century I felt I understood better, in some ways, than my own.

Chapter Fourteen

"You must be sick of me, running to you with all my troubles like this," Nora said.

I poured the coffee and pushed the jug of milk towards her. "Don't be silly. Here, have a piece of shortbread and tell me what you think — it's a new recipe with a little bit of semolina in it. I think it makes it richer."

"Mm, yes, it's delicious."

"Now then, what's the matter?"

"Well, you know I told you that in his will John asked that I should go through his papers — though why he should have imagined that I'd outlive him, seeing how much older I was. . . . Anyway, I've been putting it off; I thought it would be upsetting and I somehow didn't feel ready for that."

"That's quite understandable," I said. "Surely there can't have been any great urgency about it."

"There was, in a way. You see, the police had already been through the papers in his desk. I suppose they had to see if there was any sort of clue to his murder."

"Did they find anything?"

"I haven't heard anything from them, and when I came to look through the things in his desk and in the filing trays, there wasn't anything personal at all, only scientific stuff, papers he'd been working on, that sort of thing. No, that was no problem — I knew what he'd want me to do with *them*. There's this man at one of the teaching hospitals he's been in touch with. I'm sure he'd want me to send all that to him."

"So. What's the problem, then?" I asked.

She hesitated for a moment and then she said, "One day when I was there he showed me a little Victorian writing desk he had. A pretty thing made of walnut with a marquetry design on the lid. It seemed a very feminine thing for him to possess, but he told me that it had belonged to his grandmother, his mother's mother, and it was the only thing he had as a remembrance of her. I expect you know the sort of thing that it is — like a large box that opens up to form a writing surface with storage for pens and papers underneath."

"Oh, I know," I exclaimed. "Mother had one like that. It belonged to *her* grandmother — I gave it to Thea to give to Alice when she's grown-up. It's the sort of thing you like to keep in the family."

"I don't know about yours," Nora said, "but this one of John's had a secret compartment — not *very* secret, just a piece of wood that slides to one side and reveals a space just big enough to keep a couple of letters in."

"Splendidly romantic, like something out of a novelette — somewhere for a young lady to keep forbidden correspondence! So did you find some letters in John's?"

"There were a few old letters from his father in the main part of the desk. Brief, curt things, nothing affectionate or loving. I expect the police found those."

"But?"

"But there were several letters in the secret compartment. Two of them were from Francis Wheeler."

"Good heavens."

"I think I told you, didn't I, that something happened that made John have nothing more to do with him?"

"Yes, you did."

"Now I can see why. He did something that John found unforgivable." She paused and drank the rest of her coffee.

"What was it?"

"As I told you then, John, Virginia, and Francis Wheeler were all friends from medical school, really good friends, even after

198

they worked in different places, John and Virginia on that research team and Francis in one of the other teaching hospitals. John said that Francis was always very ambitious. He went into orthopedics because he thought he could get further quicker — apparently there were fewer people specializing in it at that time."

"Fair enough."

"As well as being ambitious in his work, Francis was very keen to get onto the social scene. There were a couple of people at his hospital who moved in those circles. You know the sort of thing I mean, young men from aristocratic families, actors, models, millionaires who'd made it young — what we'd call 'celebrities' now, I suppose. Francis was fascinated by them. He got out of his depth of course — he couldn't keep up. He wanted the lifestyle, but he hadn't got the money — he was soon in debt and borrowed from his so-called friends. He couldn't keep up in other ways too. A young doctor needs all the energy he has just to keep up with the job — especially if he's trying hard to impress his superiors."

"I can imagine. So what happened?"

"That's all John ever told me. He said it was all too squalid and he didn't want to talk about it. He was obviously upset just thinking about it, so I didn't press him."

"What about Virginia?"

"I don't think she saw Francis again while she and John were married. I don't know what happened afterwards."

"They were together at the funeral."

"Yes — it may be that John didn't tell her everything he'd heard."

"But you know now, what it was all about?"

"I managed to piece together what had happened from the letters. They were ones that Francis had written to John, with notes John had made on the back of one of the sheets."

"Good heavens."

Nora smiled. "John was a great one for making notes, even in the most unlikely circumstances."

"So what happened?"

"As I said, Francis found it difficult to keep up the pace, so he turned to drugs to keep going."

"Oh, dear."

"Exactly. He started off by buying the stuff, but when he got so deeply in debt he began stealing from the hospital. And then, to make things even worse, his so-called friends started calling in the money he owed them, and when he couldn't pay it they got him to steal drugs for them."

"How ghastly. And John found out?"

Nora nodded. "You can imagine how he felt about it, with his high standards and firm principles. Being so strong himself, he simply couldn't imagine how someone could be so weak and have gone to pieces like that."

"I can imagine."

"At first," Nora continued, "he threatened to tell the authorities what was going on, but Francis begged him not to, promised to mend his ways — all that sort of thing. Eventually John agreed not to tell anyone — though I'm sure he must have felt he was doing the wrong thing — but he insisted that Francis should resign and leave London and take a job somewhere where the social temptations were less great."

"So that's why he came down to the West Country?"

"That's right. It was a tremendous wrench, not just the social thing, but he'd been almost certain of getting a place on Sir Robert Forsyth's team — he's the top orthopedic man and it would have absolutely *made* Francis's career if he could have done that. It must have been the hardest part of all for him."

"Serves him right! So you managed to gather all this from the letters?"

"Yes, they were long rambling letters, explaining how he'd got into the mess, half trying to excuse himself and half complaining about what he called John's holier-than-thou attitude. Pathetic really."

"And John kept the letters."

"I suppose he thought they were a sort of insurance against Francis going to the bad again."

"Written proof about what had happened."

"Well, yes, I suppose they were."

"Which gives Francis a pretty good reason for killing John, don't you think?"

Nora nodded. "It's certainly a motive. But," she continued, "why now? I mean, they've both been down in the West Country for some time, so why has he waited so long?" She was silent for a moment. Then she said, "I think I told you that Francis married someone half his age. He also married well — professionally speaking, that is — his father-in-law is a top consultant and has quite a bit of influence, I believe. Perhaps Francis was planning to move up a step, go back to London even."

"That's possible."

"Even if it wasn't that," Nora said, "he

might be nervous that one day John might reveal his nasty little secret — and that wouldn't go down well with his wife's family."

"True."

"It really is a pretty powerful motive."

"Especially," I said, "since he was in Taviscombe on the day John died and he was late for the clinic at the hospital."

"Good heavens — how did you find out all this?"

I told her about my conversation with Lyn Varley. "So you see," I said, "it all mounts up, doesn't it?"

"So you think I should get in touch with your nice policeman?"

"I don't think you've any choice," I said.

The weather, which had been dull and wet, suddenly became hot and sunny again. It was stifling indoors and even in the garden the air was still and heavy. Trailing from shop to shop in Taviscombe was really enervating and I went into the air-conditioned comfort of the supermarket with some relief. I was lingering by the frozen-food cabinets, enjoying the cold air that came up from them, when I saw Alan and Susan. I noticed with envy that although every other female in the store was slopping about in brief tops or sundresses, Susan looked her usual elegant self in a neat shirtwaister.

"Hello," I greeted them, "isn't it *hot!* How do you manage to look so cool, Susan? Though I suppose after Canada you're used to hot weather."

She smiled. "Both the summers and the winters are more extreme over there."

"Do you miss it?" I asked.

"Sometimes, though I do love being back home again."

"She's always thought of England as home," Alan said fondly. "That's what she called it in her letters."

"I suppose I was always something of an expat," Susan said. "It's different for the next generation."

"Still," Alan said, "Fiona's settled down so well, you'd never think she wasn't born and bred over here. Actually, Sheila, I'm glad we bumped into you — I've been meaning to ring you. I've had an idea I'd like your opinion on."

"Really?"

"It occurred to me that it would be nice to have some sort of memorial to John Morrison."

"A memorial?"

"Yes, he was such a wonderful doctor and

he died in such tragic circumstances that I thought it would be an appropriate gesture."

"What sort of thing did you have in mind?" I asked.

"Oh, some kind of medical equipment for the hospital, don't you think? That's why I wanted to have a word with you to ask you to put it to the Hospital Friends Committee."

"Well, yes, I think that would be really nice. What do you think, Susan?"

"I agree with Alan, and I'm sure the committee will be able to come up with something the hospital needs."

"Goodness, yes, there'll be plenty of ideas, I'm sure. I'll certainly put it to them."

"Susan and I will organize a subscription," Alan said. "I daresay a lot of people will want to contribute. Mind you, I don't suppose we'll be able to raise enough for anything really big. It's just a gesture, really."

"And a very good one too," I said warmly. "Actually there's a meeting of the committee next week, so I'll let you know what they come up with. Come to think of it, why don't we use the money you raise to go with what's already been found for that new digital X-ray machine, you know, the one John Morrison came to talk to the committee about? Then it could be given to the hospital in his name."

"That's a really excellent idea," Alan said. "Don't you agree, Susan?"

"Yes, I do. It would be very suitable."

"The main thing will be to get Brian Norris on our side," I said. "He's always difficult and objects to things on principle! I don't think the others will raise any objections — oh, except Maureen Dawson, who took umbrage when Dr. Morrison wouldn't stay to have coffee with us that time. No, I'm sure there'll be a majority in favor."

Alan laughed. "Well, let me know how it goes and then we can get cracking. Fiona said she'd do some leaflet things for it on her computer — she's an absolute wonder with it, that girl. I don't know how young people keep up with things like that!"

When I got home I was about to call Nora to tell her about Alan's idea, when the phone rang. It was Thea asking if I'd babysit that evening, as they were going to supper with Jilly and Roger. So by the time I'd got myself ready, found a small gift for Alice from the store I always keep for such occasions, and seen to the animals, there was no time to get in touch with Nora.

I enjoyed my evening with Alice, who was,

fortunately, in a compliant mood and willing to be entertained, eating up all her supper, going up to bed without protest (after receiving the small gift) and even falling asleep before I'd finished my second reading of *Cinderella.* I settled down with the delicious food Thea had left for me and was so absorbed by the new biography she had also left that I was quite surprised to see them back.

"How was she?" Thea asked.

"Good as gold. No problems. How was your evening?"

"Lovely," Thea said. "Jilly did a splendid thing with halibut and a really gorgeous mango ice cream."

"Oh, by the way," Michael said, coming into the room, "Roger said he'd like to come round and see you tomorrow morning, if that's all right. Something to do with the Morrison case. I don't need to ask if you've been — how shall I put it? — taking an interest in it."

"Well, considering I was actually there when it happened," I said with dignity, "I don't think it's strange that Roger would want my input."

Michael laughed. "Input — well, that's one way of describing it. Anyway, it seems there's something he wants to talk to you about."

Roger arrived quite early the next morning. I was all behindhand anyway because Tris had upset his water bowl in the night and Foss had (probably deliberately) walked about in the resultant flood and jumped up on the work top and cooker, leaving muddy paw prints everywhere. By the time I'd finished mopping and wiping and had my breakfast and fed the miscreants and sketchily tidied up the sitting room, Roger had arrived before I'd put the coffee on.

"Sorry," I said, "I'll just go and see to it now. It won't take long."

"No, thanks," Roger said, "I mustn't stay. I've got a meeting at eleven and I must see to a few things before then."

"Well, sit down anyway and tell me what this is all about."

"Right. As you will no doubt know, I had a call from your friend Nora. She told me all about the letters she'd found from Francis Wheeler and she filled me in on the background, all the past history with John Morrison."

"Oh, good."

"I must say it was pretty damning."

"That's what we thought," I said.

"And I gather that you did your Miss Marple stuff at the hospital?"

"Yes, well, I just happened to be in there talking to Lyn Varley in reception. . . ."

Roger smiled. "I am fully aware of your methods, Sheila."

"Anyway, Francis Wheeler *was* in Taviscombe on the day of the murder and he was late for his clinic."

"Absolutely. All that is perfectly true. Nevertheless, in spite of all that, I'm afraid he couldn't possibly have murdered John Morrison."

Chapter Fifteen

For a moment I stared at Roger, not really having taken in what he said.

"What do you mean?"

"I'm afraid your case against Francis Wheeler, beautifully worked out I must say, simply doesn't hold up."

"But why?"

"Well, after you said that he had a puncture I started to think — consultant, surgeon, would need to be careful of his hands. Changing a wheel is a tricky business, could damage his hands. So I got in touch with the Rescue Services — they keep timed records of all their call-outs — and guess what?"

"What?" I asked, although I already knew the answer.

"At the time John Morrison was being murdered in Taviscombe," Roger said, "Francis Wheeler was having his tire changed by a nice RAC man just outside Crowcombe on the A358."

I sighed. "Oh, well, I suppose it was too good to be true — it all fitted so perfectly."

Roger smiled. "Life, dear Sheila, as you very well know, is not perfect."

"So have *you* any suspects, perfect or otherwise?" I asked crossly.

"Not really."

"What about alibis, then? If Francis Wheeler has one, what about all the other doctors?"

"Dr. Macdonald's in the clear. He was in his room talking to a pharmaceuticals rep. He escorted him to the door when they'd finished and he'd just gone straight into reception when that girl — Lorna — came back and told them that John Morrison was dead. The other girls, Judith Taylor, Valerie Carter and one of the nurses were there all the time, so they're all right."

"I'm glad. Though I never had Alec Macdonald down as a killer! What about the other doctors?"

"Dr. Porter was out on a call, but neither of the Stevensons have any sort of alibi. She was in her room, just come on duty, and hadn't got round to seeing her patients yet, and he says he wasn't on duty and was alone in his room working on some sort of research stuff he was doing."

"The nurses?"

"As I said, one was in reception at the relevant time and the other one was with a patient. The nurse-practitioner, what's her name?"

"Nancy Williams."

"She'd just seen one patient and she says she was checking her next patient's details on her computer when they rang through to tell her what had happened. So no alibi."

"Oh, I'm sure it couldn't have been Nancy! She's really nice."

"Niceness wouldn't necessarily be admissible in a court of law," Roger laughed.

"All right! But what motive could she possibly have had?"

"Who knows? Anyway she has to stay on the list."

I thought for a moment. "What about the people in the alternative-medicine side? They could perfectly well have come through to the surgery."

Roger shook his head. "No. All those that were in that day were with patients."

"Oh."

"However, their receptionist *wasn't* in that morning — she'd called in sick. Everyone was complaining about how difficult it made things for them. So that means the murderer could have come in that way."

"So it could have been someone from outside and not necessarily someone already in the surgery?"

"Exactly."

"Sergeant Harris did say, when he first came to see me, how difficult it was to keep track of people, given the layout of the place."

"You can say that again. No, I'm afraid the field's wide-open. It's a great pity we don't know more about John Morrison's life — apart from his work, that is." He paused and gave me a sideways glance. "I don't suppose you feel like having another chat with your friend Nora? She's about the only contact we have who could fill us in on the background and give us a few names, perhaps."

"There's his ex-wife, Virginia," I said.

"Not really. She's in London — yes, I know she could have come down to Taviscombe, but, as far as I can tell she's happily married to someone else and hasn't been in touch with Morrison for ages."

"The man she married knew him — did him a very bad turn, in fact, when they all worked together, not to mention having an affair with his wife." I told him what Nora had told me about that particular situation.

"Mm, yes, but surely it's Morrison who'd

have a motive for killing his wife and this other man, rather than the other way round."

"I suppose so," I said reluctantly.

"Anyway, she has an alibi, well, an alibi of sorts. She was in a seminar at a London hospital the afternoon of that day and it would have been very difficult for her to have made it back from Taviscombe in time."

"Oh, well, that's that."

"Cheer up, Sheila. I'm sure you'll come up with something when you've had a chat with your friend."

I didn't ring Nora straightaway after he'd gone. I felt a bit uncomfortable about it. Usually *I* approach Roger with anything I may have gleaned in the way of information. He doesn't often actually suggest that I should approach someone.

I turned out the animals' baskets, put their blankets in the washing machine and took their baskets and cushions out of doors to give them a good shake. Foss, who had been industriously digging in one of the flower beds, came up and regarded his basket suspiciously and sniffed at an old bone that Tris had hidden under his cushion and that had been dislodged by my vigorous action. Deciding that it wasn't worth investigating, he went away and sat in the sun on the lid of the cold frame at the top of the garden. Tris, however, came rushing up and claimed his hidden treasure, which he took away, with a reproachful look in my direction, to secrete it elsewhere.

Deciding I couldn't put it off any longer, I rang Nora.

"Hello," I said rather too brightly, "how are you? It's such a glorious day — I wondered if you'd like to drive out to Exford and have lunch there."

"That would be lovely."

"Splendid. I'll pick you up at about twelve, if that's all right."

Having actually made the arrangement, I felt a bit nervous until I remembered I had the good news to tell her about Alan's memorial fund. Somehow that made me feel rather better and I drove out to Porlock in a more cheerful frame of mind.

"Oh, this is nice," Nora said when we were settled in the pub. "I was feeling a bit dismal today — this is just what I needed to cheer me up."

"Well, there is something I think you'll really find cheerful," I said, and I told her about Alan's proposal.

"What a nice idea," she said gratefully.

"And I thought we could put the money raised towards the special X-ray machine he

215

wanted for the hospital and it could be in his name."

"That would be really splendid. It's something he was very keen on — in fact it was his idea that the hospital should try and get one. It would please him very much."

We had a pleasant leisurely lunch and I suggested that we should drive back over Porlock Common. The heather and the gorse were fully out and just at that peak of perfection before the first hint of brown indicates that summer is nearly over. I stopped the car on the high point from which you have a panoramic view of the surrounding purple-covered hills and a glimpse of the sea far below. A few sheep, newly released from their heavy fleeces, were industriously nibbling away at the shortgrass.

"Wouldn't it be awful," I said, looking at them, "if *we* had to forage for every mouthful of food like that? Think how your jaws would ache!"

Nora laughed. "They probably have different jaws from us — like cows with three stomachs." She undid her seat belt and opened her window. "It smells so good up here. I know I have the sea and I love the smell of that, but on a day like this up here you get that wonderful honey smell from the heather when the sun is on it. Perfect!"

"I know," I said. "Smells in certain places at certain times. It's only for a week or so that I get that wonderful smell from my balsam tree — in the spring when the leaves first come out and there's just a hint of rain in the air. That's magic."

"John always loved the spring," Nora said. "We used to go to Kew Gardens for the lilacs. I know it's a cliché, but it seemed miraculous every time." She stared out of the window, but appeared to be seeing something quite different from the scene before her. "Oh, I *do* miss him, Sheila. I thought it would get better, but it seems to be worse every day. Sometimes I don't know if I can bear it."

"Nora, my dear, I had no idea it was as bad as that. I mean, I knew you were fond of him. . . ."

"He was everything to me," she said, and the desolation in her voice silenced any sort of comforting remark I might have thought to make. We sat quietly for a while. Then she said, "He was such an amazing person. I can't begin to describe to you just how amazing."

"I know he was very brilliant. . . ."

She shook her head. "It's not just that," she said. "It wasn't just his work, though he was beginning to get back properly into his research again. He was in touch with several people in the field of genetics, people who'd always thought highly of him. He had plans —" She broke off. "I think he might have been going to America. There was an offer he was interested in. It was wonderful to see him coming alive again. It was as if he'd been in a sort of limbo and was getting back to his old self, the John I knew he could be. And then this terrible thing happened. Oh, Sheila, the *waste!*"

I nodded sympathetically.

"But as I say, it wasn't just his work. It was his whole personality, the force of his character. He had this rare gift of clarity of mind. He could go straight to the heart of any problem, whatever it was. He cut through the irrelevancies on the edge of things. He could concentrate on the essence of things."

"But not," I suggested, "in his personal relationships?"

She gave a wry smile. "I suppose they *were* irrelevancies to him. All his life people were attracted by his — his charisma, and all his life he never took any of that seriously."

"His marriage?"

"He was young when he and Virginia got married. He hadn't really set his sights on his ultimate goal. The breakup? That hit him very hard, partly pride of course, but mostly because it was betrayal by a colleague, and a colleague who'd already betrayed him over his work. That hit him harder, I think, than his loss of Virginia."

"I see."

"After Virginia he became more focused somehow. Coming down here was a conscious step towards concentrating his mind on his next move, a sort of period of calm and quiet to revive his strength before he plunged back into what for him was the real world."

"And Joanna Stevenson?"

"She was nothing," Nora said impatiently. "There had been others; there would have been others again — it meant nothing to him."

"But the baby . . ."

"That would have been an inconvenience, even if he hadn't had this thing about his father and grandfather. He would have provided for it, but if he thought she'd become pregnant to trap him, he'd never have forgiven her."

"He was a hard man," I said.

"He was a dedicated man."

"And all the others?" I asked. "The other women. Did they go quietly or did they make a fuss?"

"He was always perfectly honest with

them — told them he didn't want any sort of commitment. They didn't matter to him. Like I said, irrelevancies."

"But *they* might have had feelings. They may not have taken it as casually as he did. Don't you think one of them might just have wanted some sort of revenge?"

She smiled. "You think one of them might have come down here and killed him?"

"It's possible, surely, or a jealous husband if one of them was married — as Joanna was."

"It's just possible, I suppose, but I don't think so. The break was always clean. He chose his — his companions carefully."

"All except Joanna," I said.

"Yes, just for once he didn't realize quite what he was getting into there."

"But you don't think . . . ?"

She shook her head. "He always told me about his affairs. He told me about everything. . . ." Her voice broke and there were tears in her eyes.

"You obviously meant a great deal to him," I said.

"Yes, I thought I did —" She broke off. "But I was wrong," she said.

I looked at her in surprise. "But I thought . . ."

"Oh, yes, he cared for me in a way, but not

enough — not as I felt about him. I never expected *that* of course, but I thought he cared enough not to . . . he *was* going to America, he told me quite casually. He was going to leave England forever and he didn't ask me to go with him."

She turned her head abruptly and stared out again at the moorland and the sea below. I said nothing; there seemed nothing that I could say. Presently she turned back to me and said quietly, "You see, I loved him. It was as simple as that. And he didn't love me. For years I tried to tell myself that what I felt for him was maternal, sisterly — it was a *friendship*. And for years I managed to believe it. Being with my father helped. He never knew how I felt — I was very circumspect. John never knew. I had to be careful — I knew if he ever suspected, that would have been the end of it for me. That's why he trusted me, I suppose. He did feel for me what he never felt for all the others, but when it came to the crunch, when he was going away to start his new life, then, like all the others, I was irrelevant."

"I'm so sorry."

"When he — when he died, I couldn't tell anyone how I felt, how I really felt. People were sorry for me — poor Nora, John had been such a good friend. How could I let anyone know? John was a relatively young man and I'm an old woman — there were twenty years between us. How ridiculous I would have seemed, how pathetic. It's hard, isn't it, even in this day and age? If John had been that much older than me, no one would have thought it grotesque."

"How awful it must have been for you."

"Now there's only a sort of emptiness, and the pain, of course, that's always there. What's that thing in Shakespeare? *Antony and Cleopatra*, I think it is.

> *Young boys and girls*
> *Are level now with men . . .*
> *And there is nothing left remarkable*
> *Beneath the visiting moon.*

That's how I feel."

"He was a remarkable man. It's not surprising you feel as you do."

"That's not quite all."

"No?"

"I do have one other feeling, but it's a feeling I know I shouldn't have."

"What's that?"

She hesitated. "Underneath it all I have this awful feeling of relief."

"Relief?"

"That if I had to lose him, then it's better this way."

"I don't understand."

"If he'd gone to America, I'd always have felt that he was there, somewhere — somewhere that he'd gone where *he'd* chosen to be. Without me. As it is, he's gone, finally and forever and not by his own choice." She paused and looked at me. "Isn't that dreadful? Isn't that an appalling admission?"

I shook my head. "It's understandable," I said. "Perfectly understandable."

As we drove home, she was silent, sitting quietly like an exhausted child. When I pulled up outside her house she opened her handbag and searched for something.

"Ah, there it is," she said. "John's key. I think I'll just go and sit in his house for a while. It's the one place where I can still feel he's there. Thank you, Sheila — for everything."

I watched as she climbed the steps to his front door and stood for a moment, looking down across the bay. Then she went in and closed the door behind her and I drove away.

Chapter Sixteen

"Are you going to put anything in the flower show?" Rosemary asked.

"Yes, I'm afraid so. Ron says the dahlias should be ready and the gaillardias, and he's been growing some onions he has hopes of — they're absolutely *enormous,* and I know they'll be completely tasteless. I thought we might put the begonias in this year, but Ron wouldn't let me."

"I know he's a very good gardener," Rosemary said, "but he's dreadfully bossy!"

"I have a theory," I said. "I believe he has a fantasy that he's the head gardener of a great estate, you know, the irascible old man in books and films (usually called Mc-Gregor) who won't allow the lady of the house to pick a single rose without his say-so. Anyway, I'm not arguing. I just hope he wins something. He's even more morose when he doesn't. How about you?"

"Oh, nothing horticultural — our garden's a jungle. Jack's too busy to do much and I'm hopeless. No, I've made some greengage jam and some apple and apricot chutney — they can go in. Though I don't suppose they'll have much of a chance. Maureen Dawson always gets a first in that class for her sloe and blackberry jelly."

The Annual Flower Show signals the end of summer; it's the last social event of the Taviscombe season, which, in its way, is as rigorously structured as its London counterpart. Everyone always goes, so I wasn't surprised to see Roger there.

"Hello," I said as we met in the marquee. "What have you done with Jilly and the children?"

"Delia wouldn't come," he replied. "She said it wasn't cool — which, given the temperature in here, is literally correct, though perhaps not in the sense she meant! Alex was getting bored, so Jilly's taken him off to find some ice cream. So how about you? Have you won anything?"

"I haven't dared to look yet," I said. "But there is something I meant to ring you about."

"Hang on," Roger said, drawing me to one side, out of the way of enthusiastic gardeners, who were anxiously peering at the prize cards propped up against the exhibits. "Here's a relatively quiet spot. Now then, what was it?"

I hesitated for a moment, not sure quite how much I wanted to say. "I had a word with Nora," I said, "but I'm afraid it didn't produce much. Apparently there were other women in John Morrison's life, but no one serious, and, as far as I could gather, no one in Taviscombe. So I'm afraid it's a bit of a dead end."

"Well," Roger said, "it was worth a try. We must just concentrate on the suspects we've got. Oh, there's Jilly and Alex waving at me. I think they've had enough so I'd better go. Keep your ears open and keep me posted!"

After he'd gone I stood for a while thinking about Nora and wondering if I should have told Roger more of what I'd learned. But that would have meant betraying a confidence and I couldn't do that. And anyway, what else was there to tell him? Nothing relevant to the case, surely.

"What's so fascinating about those runner beans?" Rosemary said, suddenly appearing at my elbow.

"What? Oh — I was miles away. I suppose I'd better see how Ron's onions have done."

The onions got a second prize, though the dahlias got a first.

"Oh, dear," I said, "he's not going to be pleased, especially since it was Les Richards who got the first for onions — he does the gardens at one of the big hotels and they're deadly rivals. The dahlias didn't mean all that much to him. It was the onions he really cared about."

"Never mind," Rosemary said. "Come and have a cup of tea and celebrate the amazing fact that my apple and apricot chutney got a 'highly commended'!"

A few days later I had a call from Nora. She sounded upset.

"Sheila, can I ask a great favor?"

"Of course, what is it?"

"I had a letter from Joanna Stevenson. She said that she'd like to have a look at John's house and would I mind showing her round?"

"For goodness' sake! She's quick off the mark!"

"The thing is," Nora said, "I know it's stupid of me, but I really don't think I could face her alone. Would you very much mind coming over and being with me?"

"Not stupid in the least," I said warmly. "Of course I'll come. When is she coming?"

"Tomorrow at four o'clock. I don't think I need offer her tea, do you think?"

"Certainly not! I'll be with you at quarter to."

When I arrived Nora was very tense. She

227

waved me to a chair but didn't sit down herself, pacing the room and going to look out of the window every few minutes. I made several attempts at conversation, but she replied at random and was obviously distrait, so I gave up and we sat in silence waiting for Joanna. When she did arrive — spot on four o'clock — she was noticeably more pregnant than when I had seen her last, at the funeral. She made heavy weather of the steps leading up to John's house and when she paused on the front step she didn't turn and look at the view over the bay, but kept her eyes on the front door, watching while Nora found the key and turned it in the lock. She accepted my presence without comment ("This is my friend Sheila Malory, who is with me today") and seemed interested only in getting into the house.

"Yes," she said, looking round the sitting room, "it's barer than I remember — could do with a bit of brightening up."

I saw Nora flinch, but she said nothing.

"What I'd really like to do," Joanna continued, "is to get moved in before the baby arrives, which will be in eight weeks, if everything goes according to plan. But of course, I know I have to wait until probate is granted, which is a nuisance."

Nora still remained silent.

"Still," Joanna said, passing through into the kitchen, "I thought that if I had a good look round, I could plan things so that as soon as I *do* have probate there won't be any delay in moving in."

"You've left your husband, then?" Nora asked.

Joanna turned and looked at her, a hard, calculating look. "Yes," she said, "I have. Not that it's any business of yours." She became aware of the hatred and contempt on Nora's face and said more placatingly, "Of course I know you were by way of being a friend of John's, but our relationship was, after all, something special. I'm carrying his child — that's why he made special provision for us in his will. I'm sure he would have wanted us to be here in his house."

"There was nothing special about your relationship," Nora said steadily. "There were several before you, and had he lived, there would have been several after you."

Joanna swung round and stared at her.

"The only difference," Nora went on, "is that you foolishly got pregnant — whether by accident or design I don't know. The only thing that I do know is that John didn't want the child."

"You don't know what you're saying," Joanna said angrily.

"I expect he wanted you to have an abortion," Nora went on, "and when you wouldn't, being the conscientious person that he was, he was prepared to provide for you, in his lifetime, and, after his death, in his will."

"No — that's not true!" Joanna said, but her voice was uncertain. "What do you know about it anyway?"

Nora smiled, a pitying smile. "I knew everything about John. He was my family and I was his. After you became pregnant he didn't want anything else to do with you. Did he?"

Joanna sat down heavily on one of the kitchen chairs. "No," she said slowly, "no, he didn't. I couldn't believe it, all that nonsense about genetics. It was *his* child — how could he feel that way? I was so angry." She covered her face with her hands. When she looked up again her face was wet with tears. "He wouldn't see me or speak to me. I was desperate. I'd told Clive about the affair and about the baby — he was furious, but I didn't care. I thought John and I would make our lives together. I thought . . ." She was sobbing now, rocking back and forth.

Nora just stood there, unmoving and apparently unmoved.

I went over to Joanna and put my hand on

her shoulder. "You mustn't cry like this," I said. "It's bad for the baby. . . ."

She shook my hand off. "What does that matter now? It's all so horrible." She made a great effort and pulled herself together. "I thought — I thought, after he died and I heard about the will, he'd changed his mind. That the baby and I could live here and that would be something. . . ."

"He didn't change his mind," Nora said coldly. "However, it's your house. You are perfectly at liberty to live here if you choose. Now John has gone it doesn't greatly matter who lives here."

Joanna stared at her. "You were in love with him yourself, weren't you?"

"John was my family and I was his," Nora repeated. "It was not," she said scornfully, "the sort of love that you mean, not the sort that you could understand."

"I loved him," Joanna said helplessly. "I really did."

"But he didn't love you."

"No." Joanna shook her head slowly. "No, I don't suppose he did."

Nora gave a little nod, almost of satisfaction at having achieved this admission.

"Right, then, I'll leave you to look round." She held out the keys. "Here you are — you keep them now."

She turned and left the kitchen.

"Are you all right?" I asked Joanna. She nodded silently and I followed Nora out of the house. She was going into her own house when I caught up with her.

"Are you all right?" It seemed wrong to be asking Nora the same question I had just asked Joanna, but there was nothing else that I could find to say. "Is there anything I can do?"

"No, thank you, Sheila. It was good of you to come, but just now I think I'd be better off on my own."

"Yes, of course," I said, "I understand."

I went slowly back to my car. When I reached it I looked back. She was still standing in her front porch looking down to the sea.

The next few days I thought a lot about Nora. Several times I was on the point of ringing her, but then I decided that, given the circumstances, she'd want to be left alone. I really didn't know what to think about Joanna Stevenson. The hard, practical attitude that I had found so offensive when she was looking round the house now seemed to me a protective shield to hide a deeper hurt. She had obviously been in love with John Morrison and his attitude to the baby must have been a devastating blow to her. She said she was angry — that was only natural — but somehow I didn't think she would have been angry enough to kill him. There was, I felt, more of bewilderment and despair than anger there. She simply didn't understand what was going on. She was out of her depth. I wondered if she *would* move into John's house, or if the prospect of living so near to Nora would have frightened her away. I felt, perhaps, that it might have done. There had been something so stern and forbidding about Nora's attitude that a self-centered and rather shallow person like Joanna would shy away from. No, I thought, she would sell the house and probably move right away from Taviscombe and all its unpleasant memories.

If Joanna didn't seem to be a possible murderer — and I was pretty sure she wasn't — that really only left Clive Stevenson with any sort of motive. And Lorna, of course. We had only her word that John Morrison had been dead when she found him. There was one other possibility, but I pushed it to the back of my mind and went out shopping. I was still brooding about things when Anthea backed me up against a display of Finest Organic Produce to tackle me about the agenda for the General Annual Meeting at Brunswick Lodge.

"There's only a few weeks to go now and the thing isn't even printed, let alone distributed to the members. I knew it was a mistake to let Bruce Dawson draft it. I told you how it would be — he's let us down before — but the committee *would* ask him."

"Well," I said, temporizing, as I so often found myself doing with Anthea, "no one else seemed willing to take it on. . . ."

"Nonsense. I would have done it myself, busy as I am, if Maureen hadn't gone on about it so much that everyone had to say yes to shut her up!"

"So what do you suggest we do?"

"I thought perhaps you . . ."

"No, Anthea, I really can't. I've got so much on. What I will do, if you can get something out of Bruce, then I'll see about getting it printed and distributed."

"Well," Anthea said grudgingly, "I suppose that's better than nothing. I'll get on to him right away."

She wheeled her trolley purposefully away and I was left deeply annoyed that I'd let myself in for a tedious and burdensome task. It did turn out to be both those things because when Anthea did finally send me Bruce's draft I had to do a lot of work on it to make it comprehensible and indeed, given Bruce's strong feelings about certain aspects of the management, acceptable to the general membership. But it was a sort of distraction and when I finally got it off to the printer, I found my mind turning once again to a thought I did not want to confront.

That last afternoon with Nora had made me realize the strength of her feelings for John. Of course I'd known how she felt, had accepted that she'd felt deeply, but somehow I hadn't totally grasped the obsessive nature of that feeling. She had put him on some sort of pedestal — he had been her god, her whole life. She had accepted calmly the women in his life, as a mother would accept the minor imperfections in her child, of no importance, not relevant to her relationship with him. And he had fostered this attitude. He had recognized the intensity of her feelings for him and had encouraged them. He had allowed her to build her life around him because it suited him. I was sure that as much as he had cared for anyone, he had cared for Nora and her father. But there was something else he cared for more — and that was his work.

He had found the interlude he'd spent in Taviscombe a useful period to recover from the disasters he had suffered in London. He'd recouped his forces and was ready to move on. Although she hadn't realized it, Nora's usefulness to him was over. If he went to America — and that was where he knew he would be able to pursue what he felt was his true goal — then he would want to go without any baggage. There wasn't any place in his new life for Nora. There was probably no conscious ruthlessness in his attitude. It would never have occurred to him that it would shatter her life.

When she'd finally realized that he was going without her, when the realization that he didn't regard her as a necessary part of his life finally hit her, what would her reaction have been? Deeply upset, of course. But it was possible that she might also have been angry. After all, she'd given him so much, and it must have seemed that, to him, it had counted for nothing. She would have had every right to be angry, angry at feeling used — in the final analysis of no account.

But how angry had she been? Angry enough to decide that if John was going to destroy her life, she would destroy him? It was a possibility. Now that I'd seen the intensity of her feelings for him, I saw that it was, indeed, possible. But Nora was my friend, a very old friend, and however strong the grounds for such a thing might seem, it was somehow unthinkable that a friend could be guilty of that ultimate crime, murder.

I tried to turn my mind to other things. I went into the kitchen and emptied out the contents of the kitchen drawers and tried to restore some sort of order to their habitual chaos. Foss, as always, attracted by the sounds of any unusual activity, leaped up onto the work top to join in, and for a while, resisting his help in untangling a ball of string stuck to a roll of sticky tape, and trying to prevent him from batting onto the floor the fuses I was attempting to sort out into packets, I was able to blank out my thoughts. But when I'd got the last box of matches and packet of candles stowed neatly away, and when I'd uncrumpled and refolded the tea cloths and dusters and sorted out the cutlery drawer, when I'd done all these things, I still couldn't clear my mind of thoughts of Nora.

I gave Foss a handful of dried food to keep him quiet and then I went through to the sitting room and picked up the phone.

With the phone in my hand I still hesitated, then dialed the number. There was no reply. Only the answer phone with its bald, recorded message: "If you wish to leave a message on this number, please speak after the tone."

Chapter Seventeen

I tried phoning again later that day and then the following morning, but there was still no reply. I would have gone round there, but the copies of the agenda for the Brunswick Lodge AGM arrived and I had to spend a whole day in the committee room there with a couple of reluctant volunteers sending out copies to the members. We had just finished this exhausting task when Anthea appeared carrying a bundle of papers.

"Right, then," she said. "I've got the appeal printed."

"The appeal?" I asked.

"Yes, you know," she answered impatiently. "You must remember that we agreed to have an appeal for funds for refurbishing the kitchen."

"Yes."

"I told the printer to get a move on and I've just collected them so that you can include them with the agenda."

"But, Anthea . . ."

"I had a few more printed than we have of

the agenda so that we can leave some around here for casual visitors who might like to contribute."

"Anthea," I said, "we've done the agendas. We've just this minute finished the last ones. They're all in envelopes, sealed and with the stamps on."

"Oh, really, Sheila, this is too tiresome!"

"Well," I said crossly, "if you'd *told* us they'd be ready to be included, we'd have waited. There's no way we can do anything about it now."

One of the helpers got up. "I have to go now, Sheila, to meet the school bus."

The other one also got up and moved to the door ("I must be getting along too"), obviously unwilling to be involved in any other activity.

"I suppose you couldn't open the envelopes carefully, put in the appeal and then stick them down with Sellotape?" Anthea suggested.

"No," I said firmly, "I couldn't, nor can anyone else. I had a terrible time getting anyone to help as it was. And we can't afford the postage to send them out separately."

"Oh, well," Anthea said disconsolately, "I suppose we'll just have to distribute them at the AGM. But it's not the same."

I was so annoyed with Anthea that I

somehow didn't feel like going straight home. What I needed was a breath of sea air to blow my ill humor away. Usually I go down to the seawall by the harbor, but today I thought I'd go to Porlock Weir and then call in and see how Nora was. The tide was in when I got there, and I stood for a while watching the boats in the small harbor bobbing up and down, pulling at their moorings as if they were anxious to be up and away over the sea, which, on this sunny afternoon, reflected the sky and was unusually blue.

As I drove up to Nora's, I glanced at John's house, wondering if there'd be any signs of activity on Joanna's part, but it looked the same as usual. I rang Nora's bell, but there was no reply. I knocked and then rang again, but there was still no answer. I'd turned to go away when I saw her neighbor Mrs. Collins coming up the path next door.

"Are you looking for Nora?" she called out.

I went round to join her. "Yes, I phoned a couple of times, but there was no answer, so I thought I'd come and see if she was all right."

"Oh, yes, she's fine, but she's not here just now."

"Oh?"

"No, she's gone off to visit some friends."

"Really? She didn't mention it."

"I think it was a spur-of-the-moment thing." Mrs. Collins came closer and spoke confidentially. "She's been under a lot of strain lately with poor Dr. Morrison going like that. I think she needed to get away for a bit."

"You don't happen to know *where* she's gone?" I asked.

"Well, with friends, she said. I haven't got an address, but if you need to get in touch, she left a telephone number. I could get it for you."

"Thank you," I said, "that would be kind."

"I won't be a jiffy." Mrs. Collins let herself in and came back after a few minutes with a piece of paper. "There you are — oh, just a moment," she broke off at the sound of barking from inside the house. "I'll just go and shut Barney in. I don't like him getting out."

When she came back, I asked, "Nora left her dog with you?"

"Oh, yes, she always does when she goes on holiday. She said the people she's going to stay with have a cat and they wouldn't get on. There you are, then."

She handed me the piece of paper with a

telephone number in Nora's writing. I fished in my bag and copied the number into my diary.

"Thank you so much," I said, and gave her back the piece of paper. "You don't know how long she's going to be away, do you?"

"She didn't know, but she said she'd give me a ring before she came back so I can start the milk again for her — she canceled it before she went."

"Well, thank you very much, Mrs. Collins. I may not bother her, but it's as well to have a contact number just in case."

As I went back to my car I was puzzled. A spur-of-the-moment decision it might well have been, but I was surprised — and just a little hurt — that Nora hadn't told me she was going away.

I was busy for the next few days. Michael, Thea and Alice were away for a while visiting some friends who'd gone to live in York and I was back and forth looking after their cat, Smoke, and generally keeping an eye on things. I also had a review to do that I'd been putting off because I knew the author and couldn't think of a tactful way of saying that she'd written a terrible book. I wished passionately that I'd never agreed to do the wretched thing, but the editor of the journal who asked me was also a friend and needed it in a hurry.

I settled down at my computer and tried to think of an opening sentence but found myself instead thinking about Nora and wondering *which* friends she'd gone to stay with. The only people I could think of lived in London, and the number she had left Mrs. Collins wasn't a London number.

"The writer," Mary Russell Mitford wrote in her preface to *Our Village*, "may claim the merit of a hearty love of her subject, and of that local and personal familiarity, which only a long residence in one neighbourhood could have enabled her to attain." So it was that the circumscribed nature of her world . . .

It was no good — I couldn't concentrate on what I was writing, or rather attempting to write. What I wanted to know was not only where Nora had gone, but also why she'd gone away. *Was* it distress — did she feel she had to get right away for a while from Taviscombe and all its painful associations? Goodness knows she had every reason to feel like that. And yet . . . I felt sure that if that had been the reason, she'd have told me what she was going to do, not have disappeared like that without a word. Especially after our last conversation.

The only other explanation was one I didn't want to consider. Suddenly I felt I had to talk to her. I switched off the computer and went and found my diary with the telephone number in it. As I dialed the number I wondered what excuse I could give for phoning her. The telephone rang through for a while before it was answered, and for a moment, I was tempted to put down the receiver and forget all about it, but a voice at the other end brought me up sharp.

"Good morning, the Navidale Hotel."

"The Navidale Hotel?" I echoed in bewilderment.

"Can I help you?" It was a Scottish voice and I suddenly remembered that Nora told me that she'd once been up to the Highlands for a fishing holiday at a place called Helmsdale.

"Is that the Navidale Hotel, Helmsdale?"

"Yes, that is so." The voice sounded puzzled. I pulled myself together.

"Could I speak to Miss Nora Burton, please?"

There was a pause, then, "I'm very sorry, but we don't have a Miss Burton staying with us."

"Are you sure?" I persisted. "She's a middle-aged lady, tall, with dark hair. . . ."

"We have no ladies staying here at present, only some gentlemen for the fishing."

Another pause. "I'm sorry," I said. "I must have misunderstood. Sorry to have troubled you."

"It was no trouble," the voice said, puzzled to the last.

I put the phone down and sat staring into space. Where had Nora gone, and why had she deliberately tried to mislead people as to her whereabouts? Had she murdered John and was she now in hiding somewhere? Abroad, perhaps? There seemed no way of knowing. I could only wait until she came back. If she came back, that is. I felt I should speak to Roger, see what he thought — certainly ask if he thought there was any possibility that she was a murderer. I couldn't think — my mind was so confused. My emotions were all over the place. I got up and went out into the kitchen to make myself a cup of tea.

I'd just settled down with the tray when the doorbell rang. It was Rosemary.

"Hello, hope I haven't come at an awkward time," she said, "but I was passing the end of your lane and I thought I'd pop in and see if you felt like coming to this open-air Shakespeare thing at Dunster Castle. I've got a spare ticket. Jack was supposed to be coming with me, but he's got a meeting in Bristol that day and doesn't think he can get back in time. If you ask me," she continued, "I think he arranged it specially, amateur productions of *As You Like It* not really being his thing." She looked at me critically. "Are you all right? You look rotten."

I shook my head. "No, I feel rotten actually — something peculiar's happened. Look, come into the kitchen. I've just made some tea."

As I poured the tea and got out some biscuits, I told Rosemary about Nora going away and about the hotel in Scotland.

"Good heavens, how extraordinary!" Rosemary said. "Why on earth do you think she left *that* number?"

"I wondered that. She obviously wanted to mislead everyone — perhaps it was the first number that came into her head."

"But it wouldn't just have come into her head, not a number of a hotel she'd only stayed in once. She must have gone and looked it up."

"Perhaps," I said slowly, "it was because it was a place where she'd been happy. . . ." I shook my head. "I honestly haven't the faintest idea. Perhaps she wanted people to think she was in Scotland when she was going somewhere quite different. Abroad, even."

Rosemary looked at me sharply. "You think she may have killed John Morrison because he obviously didn't need her anymore?"

"It's possible. She was in quite a state when I saw her last — she'd obviously been bottling things up. Oh, I don't know!"

Rosemary leaned forward. "Look, Sheila, I know Nora's a friend and all that, but if you do think she killed John Morrison, then you must tell Roger. Especially now when she's disappeared."

"Not disappeared exactly," I protested.

"Disappeared," Rosemary said firmly. "I know it's difficult to believe anyone you know actually killed somebody. I didn't know Nora half as well as you did, but I know *I* find it hard to believe too. Still, if you have the faintest suspicion — and you do, don't you?"

I nodded reluctantly.

"Then," she said, "you have to talk to Roger."

"I suppose I must."

"And he's very discreet, you know that. He won't go charging into anything."

"No," I said, "you're right, of course. I knew I had to really, it's just . . . well. Just difficult." I smiled. "Thank you. You always did make me see sense when I was dithering about something."

"You mean like that time when you couldn't decide whether or not to go to the Hunt Ball with Tim Cairn-Roberts."

"That's right. I was thrilled when he asked me, but he did have that shocking reputation, and you said I'd be mad to go with him."

"And wasn't I right? He got absolutely legless and smashed the windows of the joint-master's Bentley!"

We looked at each other and laughed.

"Yes," I said, "you're right as usual. Come on, have another cup, and yes, I'd love to go to *As You Like It* with you."

I had some difficulty in getting hold of Roger the next day. He was away in London for a meeting, but he'd get in touch with me when he returned. Feeling somehow comforted that I'd set the wheels in motion, as it were, I went back to my review.

I was sitting doing some mending. It's a job I hate and one I do very badly, but when the pile of things that has to be attended to gets to a certain height, I nerve myself to get out my mother's workbox and make some sort of attempt at it. I'd just cobbled together a torn seam in a blouse and stitched back some lace that had come away from the neck of a nightdress, when the phone rang.

"Sheila, it's Roger. Can I come round?"

"Of course. When?"

"Straightaway, if that's all right with you."

"Fine, I'll expect you soon."

Thankfully I put away the workbox and my mending and tidied up the sitting room.

When Roger arrived and had sat down on the sofa I thought he seemed somehow ill at ease.

"I'm so glad you got my message and could spare the time to see me," I said. "There's something I think you ought to know."

"Your message?" Roger looked puzzled. "No, I didn't know you'd been trying to get in touch."

"Then what . . . ?"

"Sheila, I'm sorry. I'm afraid I have some bad news."

I felt that dreadful lurch of fear that you get when someone uses those particular words and your immediate thought is for your children. "Who is it?" I asked. "What's happened?"

"It's your friend Nora Burton."

I had an overwhelming and shameful feeling of relief. "Nora? What's happened to her?"

He hesitated as if not quite sure how to phrase what he had to say.

"We've found her."

"But," I said, puzzled, "I didn't know you knew she was missing."

"I'm sorry," Roger said, "I'm putting this badly. What I'm trying to say is that we found Nora Burton dead."

"Oh, God, no! Where was she? What happened?"

"She was in her car right over the other side of the moor, beyond Hawkridge. She'd driven off the road into a clump of trees — the car was quite hidden. Hardly anyone goes up there, but a farmer went to check on his sheep and wondered what a car was doing there. He found her and called us."

"So . . . ?"

"It looks as though she'd taken her own life. There was a bottle of whiskey and a bottle that had contained sleeping tablets."

I felt the tears in my throat. "How long had she been there?" I finally managed to ask.

"Several days, maybe longer. I haven't had the forensic report yet. There'll have to be an inquest of course."

"If only I'd realized," I said. "If only I'd said something, tried to help her . . ."

"Sheila, I'm so sorry — this must be a terrible shock for you. But you mustn't blame yourself. I'm sure you were a good friend to her."

"Not good enough, apparently."

"What was all this about her being missing?"

I told him about the telephone number and how I'd tried to find her.

"And all that time —" I broke off.

"You say she was in a distressed state the last time you saw her?"

"She was deeply unhappy," I said. "She obviously felt her life was finished — that it wasn't worth going on without John."

"You think that's why she did it? Grief?"

"I suppose so. That is . . ." I paused, then said, "There is another possibility, though I don't know if I can bear to think of it just now."

Chapter Eighteen

Roger looked at me. "Sheila, are you all right? Can I get you something?"

I nodded. "Yes, perhaps — it's been quite a shock. Could you pour me a glass of sherry, please — it's over there on the sideboard. Do have one too."

Roger refused anything for himself, but waited while I drank the greater part of the sherry.

"Is that better? Do you feel able to go on?"

"Yes, I'm much better. Sorry, it's just that I never imagined . . . stupid really, I should have thought — when she was so desperately unhappy."

"But you thought something else?" Roger asked.

"Yes. It's just a possibility."

I told Roger about John's plans to go to America without Nora and how upset she'd been.

"You thought she might have killed him?"

"Yes, I did. She was very bitter about it all

— that is, when she broke down and finally told me how she felt."

Roger looked grave. "As you say, it's a possibility. As good a motive as any I suppose. As good as Joanna Stevenson's perhaps."

"No," I said, "I don't think Joanna was capable of killing John." And I told him about her visit to the house and Nora's reaction. "I think she was angry and upset, but bewildered about the whole affair. Out of her depth," I said. "But I really don't think she killed him. I didn't somehow feel that her feelings were that deeply involved — I think she'll make her life elsewhere."

"You may be right," Roger said. "You mostly are, but I'll keep her on my list just in case."

A sudden thought struck me. "Roger — was there a note? Did Nora leave a note in the car or at home?"

He shook his head. "No, nothing in the car and we did go to her house of course, but there was nothing there either."

"Then she didn't kill John," I said.

"What do you mean? How can you be so sure?"

"Because if she had, she'd have left a note saying that's what she'd done. Nora was a very conscientious person. I know — I *know*

254

that if she had done it, she'd have left a note confessing so that no one else would be blamed for it."

"I see."

I put the glass down. "Such a relief," I said. "I couldn't bear to think Nora could have — silly, really. I'm sure she would have been capable of it. She may even have considered it. But she knew, I suppose, that she'd never be happy without John. I think she took the only possible way out for her."

Roger got up. "I expect you'll have to give evidence at the inquest," he said. "Evidence about her state of mind and so forth. I know it will be distressing for you, but I don't think you'll have to go into details. It's a straightforward case, no indication of foul play or anything. They'll let you know when it's to be." He looked at me. "Are you sure you're all right? Shall I ring Thea or Rosemary or anyone?"

I shook my head. "No, I'm all right. I just need a little time to come to terms with it all. Thanks all the same."

When Roger had gone I went into the kitchen and put the kettle on. The sherry was all very well, but I felt the need for a strong cup of tea. Attracted by the sound of activity, Tris got out of his basket and Foss leaped down from the windowsill where he'd been keeping an eye on the bird feeder outside the window. They sat, side by side, waiting. Confidently. Grateful for this evidence of normality, I opened a couple of tins for them.

The weather, which had been fine, suddenly took a turn for the worse — dull, cloudy and damp — and my wrist began to give me trouble. I have this inclination to arthritis — not surprising, I suppose, since my poor mother suffered badly from it — and I hoped to nip it in the bud by physiotherapy. Fortunately Jean had a cancellation and was able to fit me in the very next day.

"There's not a lot I can do if it *is* arthritis getting into the wrist where you broke it," Jean said. "But we can ease the discomfort a little." She began to assemble her equipment. "How are you? I haven't seen you for ages."

"Just ticking over. Rather sad, really. I lost a close friend recently."

"Oh, I'm so sorry, that's awful. Was it sudden?"

"Yes, it was — quite unexpected."

"That's always the worst, isn't it?"

"She was a friend of Dr. Morrison."

Jean finished putting the little pads on my wrist. "Now, that was a very strange affair," she said, switching on the machine so that I began to feel the tingling sensation. "And," she continued, "they don't seem to be much further forward in finding out who did it."

"I think they've managed to eliminate quite a few people," I said.

"Oh, really? That sergeant did come and have a word with me — had I seen anything? and so forth — but I was very busy that morning — no time to look out of the window!"

"No, I suppose not."

"Mind you, something did occur to me — oh, quite a time after — and I wondered if I should have said anything."

"Really?"

"It was about Dr. Stevenson — Clive, that is, not Joanna."

"What was it?"

"That morning I had a query about one of my patients that I wanted Clive's opinion on. I rang through and he picked up the phone and said hello, but just then another patient arrived and I had to put down the phone without saying anything. I did mean to ring him back later that morning to explain, but what with all the commotion and the police everywhere, it completely slipped my mind. Anyway, I managed to sort things out without having to consult him, so I never mentioned it to him."

"When was this?"

"Well, it was my eleven o'clock patient, but she was late — which is why I put the phone down in a hurry, so's not to waste any more time — so I couldn't be exact. But I gather it was round about then that Dr. Morrison was killed."

"It would depend how late your patient was," I said. "But I do think you ought to tell the police."

"Yes, I suppose I must, but you know how it is — you mean to do something and then time goes by and it slips your mind. To be honest, I'd forgotten all about it again until you mentioned Dr. Morrison just now."

"You lead such a busy life," I said. "You must have a great deal on your mind."

"Well, I do really, and now the boys are getting older they need ferrying about to all their sports things and with Roy and I both working . . ."

"I can't imagine how you manage it," I said.

"There are times," Jean said, "when I envy Thea, at home all day, but then I do think one should *use* one's education and training, don't you?"

There are times when Jean reminds me very much of her mother, Anthea.

I managed to get a quick word on the phone with Roger and told him what Jean had said. He sighed. "If only people would *tell* us things," he said, "but they will think they know what's important and what isn't. I'll have a word with the girl who works the switchboard at the practice — Valerie, I think her name is. She seemed quite a reliable person, I remember."

"Let me know how you get on," I said.

"Of course."

He rang me back next morning. "The girl, Valerie, confirms what your friend Jean said. She says that since the phone was put down so quickly she thought it was a wrong number so she didn't mention it. And Clive Stevenson said that when there was no reply when he answered the phone, *he* thought it was just a blip on the line — apparently they've been having some trouble with it lately. So of course, he thought there was no one at the other end of the phone who could have given him an alibi. And yes, before you ask, the time was about right. What did I say about wishing people would let us decide what's important and what isn't!"

"So Clive Stevenson's in the clear too?"

"It looks like it. And your friend Jean, too. Not that she was ever a suspect."

"So there's no one left?"

"Well, there's the girl Lorna, though I wouldn't put money on it."

"I suppose not."

"If only," Roger said with some force, "we could find the murder weapon. The shape of the wound is so distinctive — curved. I was fairly sure it had to be a surgical instrument. A curette, for instance — they come in all sizes and they're in pretty general use."

"Nothing's turned up?"

"No, and it's not likely to now. After all, we have the entire Bristol Channel on our doorstep — what easier way of getting rid of something?"

I was thinking of what Roger had said as I walked along past the harbor that afternoon. The tide was out and I gazed at the distant sea, wondering if the murder weapon was, indeed, lying somewhere out there. As I walked slowly along, trying to pick out the landmarks visible across the channel, I recognized a solitary figure leaning on the rails also looking out to sea. He didn't look up as I approached and turned only when I spoke to him.

"Hello, Alan, are you looking at Wales

too? It's really clear today. I suppose that must mean it's going to rain."

For a moment he looked at me blankly. Then recovering himself, he said, "Oh, hello, Sheila. Do forgive me, I was miles away."

I looked at him curiously. "Are you all right?" I asked. "You look really tired. Come and sit down on the seat in the shelter."

He followed me slowly and sat beside me and sighed. "Yes," he said, "I am a bit."

"You mustn't overdo things," I said. "It wasn't so very long ago that you had a major operation. Did you walk all this way from home?"

"No, I left my car just along the esplanade." He turned and faced the sea, and without looking at me, he went on. "It's not that sort of tiredness. It's more like worry."

"What's the matter? Can you tell me?"

He turned then, to face me. "It's Susan and Fiona," he said. "They've had a quarrel."

"Oh, well, mothers and daughters do, you know. It isn't the end of the world."

"It's not like that. I'm sure it's something serious."

"Do you know what it's about?"

"No — they've tried to hide it from me and when I asked if anything was wrong,

261

they said no, everything was fine and why was I asking?"

"Have you heard them arguing or anything?"

"I did, a little, a few days ago — just voices raised, but I've no idea what about, and since then, they seem to be avoiding each other. Fiona's hardly ever in now and when she is she says she's tired and goes up to her room."

"Oh, dear. I can see that would be uncomfortable for you."

"It is, Sheila. There's obviously something very wrong and I simply don't know what to do about it."

"From what you've told me," I said, "there doesn't seem much that you *can* do, except wait for them to sort things out for themselves. I'm sure they will. It's always seemed to me that they're very close, devoted to each other in fact."

Alan sighed again. "I do hope you're right," he said. "It does make me so sad to see them like this. We've all been so happy, ever since they came back from Canada — it's really given me a new lease on life."

"I'm sure things will get back to normal soon."

He got up slowly. "Well, I'd better be getting back or I'll be late for tea and I don't want to upset Susan with all this other happening."

I watched him walking slowly off towards the esplanade and wondered idly what the problem was with Susan and Fiona. They'd always seemed to me to be the ideal mother and daughter — Susan, in particular, was especially loving and protective towards Fiona. Still, no relationship is perfect and however loving it may be, it's inevitable that there will be some friction between the generations.

As it happened I saw Susan a few days later. She and Alan were at the open-air production of *As You Like It* in the grounds of the castle. They were sitting quite a distance away from us, so I couldn't have a word with her, but I was shocked to see how strained and ill she looked. Obviously whatever the argument between her and Fiona had been it was still not resolved and was affecting her badly.

"Oh, dear," Rosemary said, "do you think we were mad to come?"

I looked at her inquiringly.

"Well, you know how it is with things out of doors in the evening. Either it's a nice warm evening and you get bitten to pieces by midges, or it's cold and damp and you freeze to death."

"It's quite warm this evening," I said consolingly.

"Too warm really, and we're so near the river — the midges will be out in full force."

"I think I may have some insect repellent in my bag."

"It's no good," Rosemary said despondently. "I'm allergic to most of them."

It was a charming production by very good amateurs, and Rosemary had cheered up enough by the interval to agree that a glass of wine would be a splendid idea.

"I'll go," I said. "There's no need for us both to stand in the queue."

"All right, if you're sure. Actually I want to have a word with Maureen — she's sitting a couple of rows back — about some plants she promised me."

I was pleased to see that Susan was just in front of me in the queue for refreshments.

"Hello," I said "are you enjoying it?"

"Oh, yes," she said, "it's very good." Her tone was abstracted as if she was speaking at random.

"I thought the girl playing Rosalind was excellent," I said, "almost up to professional standards. And the man doing Touchstone was marvelous — I think I've seen him with the opera group when they were doing a Gilbert and Sullivan."

"Really?"

"How are you all?" I asked. "How's Fiona?"

"Oh" — she focused her attention on me at the name — "she's fine. Busy, you know."

Alan came up and joined us. "Hello, Sheila, nice to see you. Actually I wanted to have a word. Can you manage lunch next Friday? Alec Macdonald said he'd come and have a word about this new machine the Friends are raising money for, you know, the one we were talking about."

"Well," I said, "I'd love to come, but I'm not sure if I can make it. The thing is I have to give evidence at an inquest that morning and I'm not sure how long it will take."

"An inquest?" Alan asked. "That sounds serious."

"Yes," I said, "it's very sad. A friend of mine, Nora Burton, I don't think you know her."

"No, what happened?"

"I'm afraid she committed suicide."

"What a dreadful thing — what happened?"

"She was a great friend of John Morrison," I said quietly, "and when he was killed she — well, she just didn't feel able to go on without him."

"But that's terrible!" Susan spoke very loudly, so that the people in the queue in front of us turned round and looked at her curiously.

"Yes," I said, "it was a great shock. Such a waste — both of them really, two very valuable lives wiped out like that."

"You're a friend of that detective, aren't you?" Alan asked. "Do you know if they're any nearer finding out who did it?"

"I don't know," I said. "It all seems so complicated."

"Well, look," Alan said, "about next Friday — come when you can. Even if you can't manage lunch, we can still have a chat."

We'd reached the head of the queue now and I bought our glasses of wine and went back to join Rosemary.

"Sorry you had to queue for so long," she said, taking a sip of the now rather warm Chardonnay. "Was that Susan Campbell you were talking to? What on earth's the matter with her? She looks awful!"

"I think there's some trouble between her and her daughter," I said, "that seems to have upset her badly."

"Poor soul," Rosemary said, "children

can be an endless worry. Did I tell you that I had a letter from Colin saying that he's thinking of taking a job in South America! I mean, not that I've anything against South America as such. It's just that it seems even *farther* away than Canada, and sometimes I feel I'll never get to see him again!"

Chapter Nineteen

I'd had a particularly irritating and exhausting afternoon. Right after lunch Anthea phoned to ask me to do a number of things for which I had neither the time nor the inclination, but because Anthea always tanks over any objections I may raise and (to be honest) because I'm too feeble to stand up to her, I found myself landed with a number of small but tiresome jobs. Probably because of the irritation this provoked, I knocked over a bottle of milk that went all over the kitchen floor, spreading like a tidal wave and needing to be mopped up very thoroughly because nothing smells so vile as decaying milk. This also led to Tris, who was outside wanting to come in, whining pathetically at the back door because I didn't want milky paw marks all over the house, while Foss, alerted by the sound, sat on the kitchen windowsill, craning his head to see if there was anything in the way of entertainment going on inside.

When I'd got all that cleared up and the

animals pacified with food, I thought I'd better sort out the tins for recycling. Our local council now insists that we separate our tins, wash them out and squash them into a convenient state for collection, a job I hate. Resentfully I was engaged in this task when I cut my hand on the jagged lid of a cat food tin. It wasn't a bad cut, but it was in an awkward place and bleeding fairly profusely. I held it under the cold tap for a bit and put on some antiseptic cream, but when I reached for the packet of plasters I found it was empty, so I had to trail all the way upstairs to get one from the bathroom cabinet. While I was up there I smelled burning and came down to the kitchen to find that the potatoes I'd put on after Anthea phoned had boiled dry, so I had to throw them away and put the blackened saucepan in the sink to soak.

I decided I couldn't be bothered to do any more and that I'd just have bread and butter with my lemon sole. After all that, I felt I deserved a little rest so I took a bar of chocolate and switched on the television to watch *Antiques Roadshow*, a program I always find very soothing. There were the usual collection of people and things, the elderly with objects that they had "found in the attic after Mother died" or that had "been in the family for many years" and the young with things they'd bought at sales or had "been left me by my auntie" — small silver objects, not-quite-right Regency tables, Victorian watercolors, "collectibles" (which can mean virtually anything nowadays), with the occasional "find," some rare item of actual value. The owners of these things listened, rather dazed, to the experts pronouncing on their possessions, and waited with suppressed eagerness for the magic moment when an actual price was given.

I was meditating on this when my attention was caught by one of the objects and what the expert was saying about it.

"A dagger of Middle Eastern origin, quite a fine specimen, notice the intricate chasing on the sheath. It is what is known as a *jambiyeh* and is a high-status object, often given as a gift or token. When I take it out of the sheath you will notice the curved blade — very sharp, as you see. You may remember having seen such an object in the film of *Lawrence of Arabia*. . . ."

I sat there not listening anymore. I had certainly seen such an object not so long ago, in a glass case in a drawing room in Taviscombe. For a while I couldn't take in the implications of this, and then, I tried to blur the picture that was forming in my mind. Taviscombe was full of retired people, people, no doubt who had been abroad, who had come back with souvenirs of their time there. Colonel Wilmot, for example, had a collection of ebony elephants and several brass tables that he'd brought back from India; Patrick May had a couple of primitive wooden masks, a reminder of his days as an anthropologist in West Africa. There may well have been others besides Alan Johnson who had come home to Taviscombe from somewhere in the Arab world.

I knew this was nonsense, though. What was staring me in the face was the fact that the weapon that had killed John Morrison — or one like it, though that would surely be too much of a coincidence — belonged to Alan and had been available to any member of that household. It *couldn't* have been Alan. He'd always spoken so highly of John, was even now arranging for a memorial to him at the hospital. Of course that could all have been a front, hiding his real feelings, but then, what on earth would have been his motive? Susan too had no reason to dislike him and, although not as overtly enthusiastic as her brother, was equally full of praise for him, especially after he'd been so good over Alan's heart condition.

That left Fiona. But there again, what

could have been *her* motive? I could remember her saying several times how good he'd been to her uncle and how he'd virtually saved his life. No, the whole thing was inexplicable. The only thing I knew I had to do was tell Roger about the dagger so that it could be tested for traces of blood or whatever they do to murder weapons. But — I was brought up short — how could I do that without seeming to accuse my friends?

I spent a wretched night, waking up in the small hours and going over and over the problem in my mind. By the morning I felt I couldn't bear the burden of it any longer and phoned Rosemary and asked her to come round.

"What on earth's the matter? You sounded dreadfully agitated," Rosemary said when she arrived. "Are the children all right?"

"No, it's not that. It's more a moral dilemma."

"Oh," Rosemary said, looking relieved, "one of them."

Briefly I told her what I'd seen on the television and about the similar dagger that Alan had.

"So you see," I said, "I must tell Roger about it, but then, if I do, where does that leave Alan and Susan?"

"Perhaps someone could have got into the house and taken it," Rosemary suggested.

"*And* put it back again? I'm sure they would have missed it if it had gone."

"I suppose," Rosemary said tentatively, "it *could* have been one of them, or Fiona."

"But why! It just doesn't make sense. They're our friends — we've known them for ages. What possible reason could any of them have for doing something like that?"

Rosemary shrugged. "People do peculiar things. No, I think you have to tell Roger, no matter what."

"It will be awful," I said, "especially now when there's all this bother between Susan and Fiona —" I broke off suddenly. "You don't think," I said, "that had anything to do with all this?"

"With John Morrison's murder? Surely not."

"But they've always been so close — Alan simply couldn't understand it, and they wouldn't tell him what the problem was. But if Fiona . . ."

"But *why?* And why would they fall out now?"

I shook my head wearily. "Who knows? No, you're right. I must tell Roger about the dagger and if Alan and Susan never speak to me again, so be it."

But when I tried to phone Roger they said he was in London again and could anyone else help me? I hesitated for a moment and then said I'd ring again when he was back. I kept going over and over all the possibilities of the situation and, eventually, the impossibilities, but I still couldn't make any sort of sense of it. Finally, I resolutely tried to put the whole thing to the back of my mind and, as a sort of penance, concentrated on doing all the things Anthea had asked me to do for Brunswick Lodge.

I'd brought back with me a list of people who had to be told about a change Anthea wanted made to the arrangements for an exhibition about old Taviscombe she wanted to stage — committee members and members of the local history society — and prepared to concoct some sort of circular letter ("It's easy for you — you can just do it on that computer of yours"). I made myself a cup of coffee and banished the animals from my study, since they hate my using the computer, and was just settling down to work when the phone rang.

It was Alan and he was very agitated. "Sheila, something terrible's happened!" He sounded breathless and distressed.

"What is it?"

"It's Susan — she's dead."

"What!"

"It's really terrible, a dreadful thing —" He broke off, obviously trying to catch his breath.

"Alan, calm down. Take it slowly. What's happened?"

There was a pause while he tried to collect himself. "I'm sorry," he said at last. "It's all been such a shock. I'm at the hospital. Susan was knocked down by a car. They got an ambulance, but she was — she was dead when they got her here."

"Oh, Alan, I'm so sorry. That's really appalling. Is Fiona with you?"

"No, she's in Taunton and I can't get hold of her. I hope you don't mind my calling you, but I couldn't think who else to ring. . . ." His voice trailed off.

"I'll come over right away," I said. "Hold on."

When I got to the hospital I saw Sandra Bradshaw, one of the Sisters, in the foyer and asked if she knew where Alan was.

"I put him in the consultant's office. I'll show you. Poor soul, he's in shock. He'll be glad to see you."

Alan was sitting slumped in a chair, an untouched cup of tea on the desk in front of him.

"Here's Mrs. Malory for you," Sandra said. "Now drink up that tea — it'll do you

275

good — and I'll send Dr. Macdonald in to see you as soon as he comes in."

He really did look awful, old and frail.

"Sandra's right," I said. "Drink the tea — they've probably put masses of sugar in it, but it will help." Like an obedient child he drank the tea. "That's better," I said. "Now can you tell me what happened?"

"It was that crossing at the bottom of West Street — you know, we've always said how dangerous it is. A car came round — hadn't indicated, you know how they don't there — Susan must have thought it was going straight on down the Avenue and stepped out right in front of it and it couldn't stop in time. . . . Several people saw it happen. They called an ambulance, but" — his voice broke — "it was too late."

I put my hand over his. "I'm so sorry," I said quietly, "so very sorry."

Sandra came back into the room with Alec Macdonald. "Here's Dr. Macdonald, who'll give you the details."

"I'll go and phone Fiona's office," I said to Alan, "and ask them to tell her. Will you be here until then?" He nodded and I went away.

I rang Fiona's office and told them what had happened and they said they'd get through to their Taunton office and tell her to come back right away.

"Her uncle's at the hospital now," I said, "but I'm going to try and persuade him to go home, so perhaps she could go straight back there."

When I got back to Alan, Dr. Macdonald had gone.

"He said it was almost instantaneous," Alan said. "He doesn't think she would have suffered. I suppose that's a mercy."

"A great mercy," I said. "Look, Alan, I think you should go home. There's nothing you can do here at present. Her office is going to tell Fiona to go straight home. I thought that was best."

"Yes, whatever you think, Sheila."

I drove him home and sat him down in the drawing room with a glass of brandy, trying to make some sort of conversation.

"You'll stay until Fiona comes, won't you, Sheila?" he asked anxiously. "I really don't know how she'll take it — after the way things have been between them. . . ." His voice trailed off and he sat nursing his glass and staring at the empty grate.

"Of course I will," I said.

We sat in silence for a while and I couldn't help my eye's straying to the cabinet. The dagger was still there, sitting innocently beside the other richly decorated objects. It seemed impossible that it could have been used for such a terrible purpose. I tried to divert my thoughts, feeling I shouldn't be even speculating about it at such a time.

After what seemed like an age I heard the sound of the front door opening, and Fiona came into the room. She came in slowly, as if reluctant to face what she already knew had happened. Alan got slowly to his feet and held out his arms to her. For a moment she seemed to hesitate and then she clung to him, silently, no tears, but her face, over his shoulder, was twisted with grief.

I went out into the kitchen. There seemed nothing I could do except the conventional thing of putting on the kettle and making tea. When I took the tray into the drawing room they were sitting side by side on the sofa, Fiona's arm around his shoulder. He was in tears, but she was not.

"I thought you might like some tea," I said inadequately. I poured them each a cup. "I'll leave you alone now, but please do call me if there's anything at all I can do."

"Thank you so much, Sheila," Fiona said. "That's very good of you."

When I got home I phoned Rosemary to tell her the news.

"Poor Susan. How dreadful! We always said there'd be an accident there, but what a horrible way to be proved right! How's Fiona taking it?"

"She seems very calm — strangely so, considering how close they were."

"I don't suppose it's really sunk in yet," Rosemary said.

"I sort of wondered — after the trouble between them . . ."

"Whatever it was, Susan was her *mother* after all. She's bound to be really upset. How about Alan?"

"He just seemed bewildered at first — it must have been the most awful shock to him, happening so suddenly like that — but he broke down when Fiona got back. She was very good with him."

"It's a blessing they've got each other."

"Yes, family's very important at a time like this."

We were both silent for a moment, considering this. Then Rosemary said, "I suppose you haven't phoned Roger — you know, about the dagger?"

"I did try, but he's away for a few days and now, of course . . ."

"I know. It hardly seems the time, does it?"

"It was awful," I said. "When I was with Alan, I couldn't help looking at the wretched thing in its glass case. I wish to goodness I'd never *seen* that television thing."

"I wonder," Rosemary said slowly, "I wonder if —"

"What?" I asked.

"Susan, if it wasn't an accident."

"You mean, did she do it deliberately?"

"It's possible — that is, if she did kill John Morrison." She stopped short. "Oh, dear, it's awful to be talking like this. Still, you can't help wondering."

I found I was doing quite a bit of wondering myself, speculating about what might have happened, and then pulling myself up short and thinking of what Alan and Fiona must be going through. The following day I phoned Alan to see how they were.

"Fiona's gone to work," he said. "I wanted her to stay at home, but she said she'd be better doing something."

"How is she?"

He sighed. "I really don't understand it — she hasn't cried once. She seems quite calm, but not really *here,* if you know what I mean."

"I suppose she hasn't really come to terms with what's happened."

"In denial? Is that the phrase they use

nowadays? Honestly, Sheila, I could cope with it better if she did break down."

"I know. I suppose," I said, "that there'll have to be an inquest because it was an accident."

"Yes, the police have been in touch. Actually, because it's all quite straightforward — there were several witnesses, you know — I may be able to go ahead with actually making the arrangements. Though, of course, we can't fix a date yet."

"That would be a good thing. As Fiona says, it does help to have something to do."

"Poor Susan," Alan said, "I'm going to miss her so much. You know, it seemed like a miracle when she came back, after all those years, and with Fiona too. I still can't believe she's gone." His voice broke and with a brief good-bye he put down the phone.

Whatever I tried to do that day, I found my mind constantly going back to Susan and Fiona and John Morrison — and the dagger. I wished Roger would come back so that I could lay at least part of my burden of worry on him.

The following morning, Alan phoned. He sounded very agitated and for a moment I couldn't understand what he was saying. Then he collected himself and said, "I've just been into Morgan and Phillips, you know, the undertakers, and something very peculiar has happened. I don't want to talk about it on the phone, Sheila, but could you come round right away?"

Chapter Twenty

When I drove up to the house I saw Alan standing by the window, waiting for me to arrive. He ushered me quickly into the drawing room and said again, "Something very peculiar's happened."

"What is it?"

"Well, I told you the police said I could see about the funeral, so I went to see Mr. Phillips this morning. He's very helpful and nice — he did the arrangements for poor Mary when she passed away."

"Yes, I know him quite well."

"I wanted to have a word straightaway to let him know that it would have to be a burial, not a cremation — which is what we had for Mary and what I want for myself as a matter of fact. The thing is, Susan had a pacemaker and apparently they explode if the — the body is cremated."

"Yes, I had heard that. But I'd forgotten that Susan had one."

"She was very sensitive about it — goodness knows why. You know they put them in on the chest — that's why she always wore high necks. She used to go up to Taunton to the hospital every three months to have it checked and adjusted."

"They're amazing things," I said. "They seem to keep people going wonderfully well. It must have been difficult for Susan, problems with her heart."

"It runs in the family. Our father and our grandfather both died of heart conditions and our mother's sister and her brother. I had a long conversation with Dr. Morrison about it once — you know he was a specialist in genetics — and he was most interested. Anyway," he continued, "I was explaining all this to Mr. Phillips when he brought me up short by saying that Susan didn't have a pacemaker."

"Good heavens."

"Well, I couldn't believe it. I asked if there were signs of it having been taken out or dislodged in some way by the accident, but he said no, there was no sign that there'd ever been one."

"That is extraordinary. You're sure she had one?"

"Well, of course I am," Alan said shortly. "I remember her telling me about it in one of the very first letters she wrote to me after she got in touch again. She'd just had it fitted and I wrote back to say wasn't it wonderful the way things had improved? Because our aunt had had her first bad heart attack when she was just about the same age as Susan, and of course, there wasn't anything like a pacemaker then."

"Did you actually *see* it?"

"Well, no, I don't suppose I did. As I said, Susan was sensitive about it, and anyway, it's implanted under the skin."

"Have you asked Fiona?"

"She's back at work — I think I told you. But I was so upset — it's all so extraordinary — I felt I had to talk to someone about it, and you've always been such a good friend to us both. . . ."

"Of course. I just wish I could help, but honestly, I can't think of any sort of explanation."

"I'll just have to wait, then," he said, looking downcast, "until Fiona gets back."

I looked at my watch. "It's almost twelve thirty," I said. "Let's go out and have lunch — you have to eat something. Why don't we go down to Porlock Weir to the pub there? The drive will do us both good."

He brightened up a little. "That's a good idea. Then we could have a little walk by the sea. Perhaps the breezes will clear my head and help me make sense of all this."

We had our lunch at the Ship and went for a walk by the sea. As we stood by the little harbor I looked up at the hillside at Nora's and John's houses and thought about them and about Susan — and about the dagger in its glass case.

"What time will Fiona be back?" I asked.

"About five," Alan said. "It's usually later, but they said she could work a shorter day, under the circumstances."

"Well, look," I said, "it's a lovely day — let's go for a little drive along the coast. We might go as far as Lynmouth."

"Yes, I'd like that."

So we drove over the moorland, skirting the sea, neither of us saying much, but comforted somehow by the timeless contours of the countryside with the gorse and heather in full bloom. It was nearly five o'clock when we got back to Alan's and I offered to make a cup of tea for us all. While I was in the kitchen I heard Fiona come in and Alan call out to her. I took as long as I could with the tea to give them time to talk and then I carried the tray into the drawing room.

"Can you think of any explanation?" Alan was saying. "It's beyond me."

Fiona was sitting in a chair with her back to the window and when I first came in I couldn't see her face, but as I moved to a chair beside her I saw that she was dreadfully pale and obviously in great distress.

"Fiona, what is it!" I hadn't meant to say anything, merely to pour the tea and leave them alone together, but she looked so terrible I couldn't help myself. She'd been looking at her uncle, but she turned to me, I thought, almost gratefully.

"I have to explain," she said dully. "It's time it all came out. I wanted to before, but she wouldn't let me, but now . . ." She made a vague gesture, apparently of despair.

"What on earth do you mean?" Alan cried. "Who wouldn't let you?"

"I'll leave you to talk," I said, moving to the door.

"No!" Fiona almost shouted. "No, please, Sheila, please stay."

"Yes," Alan echoed, "please stay."

I sat down and waited for Fiona to continue. She sat silently for a while, her hands grasping the arms of her chair, and then she burst out, "It's all been a sham — I feel awful about it — you've been so wonderful to us and now . . ." She paused and shook her head as if to clear it and went on. "I suppose I'd better start at the beginning." She turned to Alan. "My mother wasn't your sister and I'm not your niece."

"I don't understand," Alan said. "What do you mean?"

"Susan Campbell was a lovely person," Fiona said, "and Mother and I owe her so much." She paused again. "This is so difficult, I don't know how to put it. Mother's name was Phyllis Lucas — I'm Felicity Lucas — my father left us when I was a baby, so she took what jobs she could where she could keep me with her. That's how she ended up as housekeeper to Susan Campbell. Susan was delighted that Mother had a little girl because she had a daughter the same age and she thought it would be nice for her to have a companion. Her husband had died fairly recently and she wasn't very well — she had a heart condition — and she wanted someone to look after the house and — well, things in general. She soon came to rely on Mother — they got on really well together, just as Fiona and I did. Fiona and Fi (I was always known as Fi), 'just like sisters,' Susan used to say."

She got up and began to walk about the room.

"One of the things Susan used to like to do was to talk to Mother about the old days in Taviscombe — she'd get out photos and talk about the family, the house where she was brought up, old friends, things like that.

It was obvious she missed them very much. Mother used to say, 'Why don't you go over there to see them?' But Susan was terrified of flying, and then there was her heart. . . . So Mother got her to write to you, to make contact again, and then you wrote back and she was so happy about it all. It was about then that she saw a specialist about her heart and they fitted her with a pacemaker. That improved her health no end, but she still relied on Mother, said she could never manage without her. But she did start to do things again, like driving and going to the cinema, things like that."

She stood for a moment by the window, looking out. Then she turned and went on.

"One of the things Susan had always wanted to do was to live in Montreal. Her husband had always lived in Toronto — that's where his work had been and his friends (he had no family) — so she'd never been able to. But one day she saw an advertisement in a Montreal newspaper for this house, and without even seeing it, she made an offer for it and it was accepted. Mother made all the arrangements, of course, and saw to the move — she was very efficient about things like that, as you know. Well, we'd only been in Montreal for a week when it happened." She came and sat down in the chair beside me and said, "It was the handbags that were responsible for what happened."

I looked at her in astonishment. "The handbags?" I echoed.

She nodded. "Susan had a very nice brown leather handbag that Mother always admired, so for her birthday Susan bought her one just like it. Sometimes they used to get them mixed up — they always made a joke about it — and that's what happened that day. Susan and Fiona had gone shopping. The house in Montreal was a little way out of town and you had to take a rather busy road to get to the shops. There was an accident — a truck ran into their car." She sat silently for a moment and then went on. "The policeman who came said, 'I'm afraid I have some bad news. Mrs. Phyllis Lucas and her daughter have both been killed in an accident.' Susan had taken Mother's handbag by mistake and that led to the confusion. Mother started to correct him. Then, suddenly, on an impulse, she didn't. She let him think that she was Susan."

"Good God!" Alan said.

"I'm sorry," she said. "I'm truly sorry. Anyway," she went on, "it was unbelievably simple. No one in Montreal knew who we were — Fiona and I hadn't started school — Mother had made all the arrangements. Susan had arthritis in her hands, so she typed her letters on an electric typewriter." She turned to Alan. "She typed those to you. Her signature was easy to copy. So we went on for a bit. Then Mother began to get nervous — she thought someone might turn up from Toronto and recognize her. Then when she heard that your wife had died, she decided that it would be safer to come to England. To help look after you, she said in her letters, because she'd kept up the correspondence. There were no pictures because Susan always hated having her photo taken and she never got around to having one done of Fiona. It wasn't too much of a gamble. You hadn't seen her since she was a child, and she and Susan were much the same age and had the same coloring. You were expecting Susan, so you didn't suspect anything."

Alan shook his head but didn't say anything.

"So that's how it was. We came to live with you and you were so good to us. I'm so sorry. . . ." Her voice broke and she was crying. No sobs, just silent tears. She looked pale and exhausted.

Alan was still silent. He looked as if he

hadn't taken in half of what Fiona — Felicity — had been saying.

"You and your mother were very close, especially after all you've — all you've been through," I said gently. "Her death must have been a dreadful shock to you."

She shook her head. "It's so awful. I said I couldn't forgive her for what she'd done — it was too much. She died while I was still angry with her and now she'll never know how much I loved her."

"What couldn't you forgive her for?" I asked quietly. "Killing John Morrison?"

She turned towards me, a look of shock and disbelief on her face. "How did you know?" she asked.

"I worked it out," I said. "About the dagger. I didn't know why, though, until today. John Morrison found out somehow, I suppose."

She nodded. "Uncle Alan . . ." She paused and corrected herself. "Alan had told Dr. Morrison about the pacemaker, but she didn't know that, and when she went to see him about her bronchitis and he sounded her chest, he mentioned the conversation and asked her about it. She made some excuse, about having had it removed, but he was obviously suspicious. That's when she decided to kill him — she said she couldn't risk him talking to Alan about it."

"But surely," I said, "there's patient confidentiality. . . ."

"She wouldn't risk it. She was in a panic — she wasn't thinking properly. She just thought that everything would blow up in her face. She said she took the dagger from the case and put it in her shopping bag. There was no one on duty at the alternative-medicine entrance, so she simply walked round the quadrangle to his room. There's a treatment room next door, so she hid in there until she heard a patient leaving. Then she went in and — and killed him, and went out the same way and walked into the waiting room and sat down beside you, Sheila."

I remembered Susan — Phyllis — sitting chatting with the shopping bag at her feet, the shopping bag that had presumably contained the dagger covered in John Morrison's blood, and I shuddered.

"When did you find out — about the murder, I mean?" I asked.

"Just a few weeks ago. I had no idea. . . . I don't really know why she told me then. I suppose bottling it up for so long, she felt she had to tell somebody. I was the only person she could tell."

"It must have been a terrible moment for you," I said.

"I couldn't believe it — I said, '*Why* did you have to do that! We could just have gone away, started somewhere else.' She said she did it for me, that she'd done everything — the whole deception — for me. But how could she think I'd want that! When she heard from you about your friend, the one who killed herself, that shook her very much. I think it was the first time it really came home to her what she'd done."

"You don't think," I said, "that her own death wasn't an accident, that she stepped out in front of that car deliberately?"

She covered her face with her hands for a moment. Then she looked up and said, "It's been going round and round in my head — I honestly don't know. Anyway, what does it matter now? She's gone. . . ." The tears came again, silent, hopeless tears.

"You'll have to go to the police," I said.

"I know. It'll all come out now, the whole miserable business. Everyone will know how we've lied and cheated. That will be the end of it for me and Phil — he'll never speak to me again — how could he." She turned and faced Alan. "I've got some money saved up, enough for Mother's funeral. If you could just let me stay here a couple of days until I can find somewhere else — I'll keep out of your way. I know how you must hate me."

"No!" Alan burst out. "Don't be ridiculous — of course you can stay here. How could you think otherwise? I don't deny," he went on more quietly, "that it's all been a bit of a shock. But the deception, as you call it, that was nothing to do with you — you were just a child. It was wrong, of course, but if only she'd told me, we could have worked something out — you've been like family to me, even if you weren't. I've come to rely on you both, become fond of you. When I was ill you both looked after me so wonderfully well. I wouldn't be here now if it wasn't for you."

"And Dr. Morrison," she said quietly.

"Yes, well, that was a terrible thing, but, poor soul, she paid the price for it in the end. Sheila's right, we have to go and see the police — I'll come with you."

"No, no," she said through her tears, "it's too much — I don't deserve it."

"Come on, now," Alan said, "let's see what's to be done. First thing, we'll have a cup of that tea Sheila made before it gets stone-cold." He smiled at me and I got up and poured the tea.

"Roger Eliot is very discreet," I said. "I'm sure he won't reveal more than he has to about the situation. After all, it's an open-and-shut case now."

"Exactly," Alan said. "People will gossip for a while, but if you're still here and you still call me Uncle Alan — and I hope you will, Fi — then they won't have anything much to gossip about, will they?"

On my way home I thought a lot about how Alan had taken what was, after all, an appalling situation. His reaction to it and what appeared to be his easy acceptance once again of what had been the status quo seemed vaguely shocking. After all, Susan — Phyllis — had murdered someone, a distinguished and valuable member of the community, and although Alan had made the right conventional noises, he hadn't shown any personal expressions of condemnation. But the more I thought about it, the more I realized that, at his age, the important thing *was* the status quo, and that although he'd been shaken and distressed at the deception and the murder, what he really wanted was for things to go on as they had been and that his way of life — given a few interruptions, a court case, an inquest — would continue that way until the end, and if that meant ignoring certain unpleasant facts, so be it.

★ ★ ★

The raven was back. I saw him moving slowly across the lawn, the other, lesser birds making room for him, like courtiers falling back to ease the progress of their sovereign. He stood there, looking about him, and his confidence, self-assurance and assumption of effortless superiority reminded me somehow of John Morrison. On an impulse I opened the back door and went out to have a closer look. To my surprise he didn't move, but stood looking at me, eye to eye. The raven, harbinger of death, said the legend; nevermore, said the poet. I took another step forward and slowly he rose in the air and flew majestically away.

About the Author

Hazel Holt was a personal friend and literary adviser to Barbara Pym, and is Pym's official biographer. A former television critic and feature writer, she lives in Somerset, England.

The employees of Thorndike Press hope you have enjoyed this Large Print book. All our Thorndike and Wheeler Large Print titles are designed for easy reading, and all our books are made to last. Other Thorndike Press Large Print books are available at your library, through selected bookstores, or directly from us.

For information about titles, please call:

(800) 223-1244

or visit our Web site at:

www.gale.com/thorndike
www.gale.com/wheeler

To share your comments, please write:

Publisher
Thorndike Press
295 Kennedy Memorial Drive
Waterville, ME   04901